Valley of Shadows

Valley of Shadows

by

Charles Hawkins

Blorenge Books
1997

ISBN 1 872730 14 0

Cover design by Michael Blackmore

Blorenge Books, Church Lane, Llanfoist,
Abergavenny, Gwent NP7 9NG. Tel: 01873 856114

Printed by Mid Wales Litho Ltd.,
Units 12/13, Pontyfelin Industrial Estate,
New Inn, Pontypool, Gwent NP4 ODG

* * * * * *
For my mother

* * * * * *

All the names used in this story are of actual people, but except for the family, not necessarily in context. They all somehow or another touched the life of Annie May Chappell (1891-1975).

CHAPTER ONE

The town clung for dear life to the sides of the deeply etched valley. Long rows of miners' cottages sprawled for almost twenty miles, North to South, a ribbon of towns bred from the black diamond buried beneath, ten million years before.

But Annie May dwelt not on these things. She had Sunday afternoon off from service in the Meyrick's household and her eyes reached for the summit of Domond Fawr, except when she stopped and stooped to wonder at the strong veins of hillside fern or turned her head the better to hear the music of the birds and the scurry of tiny mountain creatures. There were rare patches of Forget-me-knots, but they were not for picking, and the hardy wimberries were not ready so Annie May enjoyed the sight of them and travelled ever upwards to the ridge, wondering how the straggly Welsh sheep managed to climb so much more easily than she did.

The mountain that Annie May was climbing had not seemed so immense from down below, but as the climb tugged at her breath and her stamina, she realised how wrong she had been. The last hundred feet turned her legs to jelly and her breathing rasped its objections. She flopped onto the ridge and it was some minutes before she could sit up and then stand to wonder at the majesty of all those other hills and peaks reaching upwards in distant places.

When she had filled herself with landscapes, she sat and looked where she had come from. Christchurch tower thrust itself high above the town and there was the chapel and the Meyrick's villa. "Nice lady Mrs. Meyrick", she spoke aloud, "and Mister is nice too. There's the Council Offices where he works. Nice of her to give me an apple for my walk", she said taking the rosy fruit from the drawstring bag. As she munched, her eyes followed the Dram Road and from her grandstand view, she could make out The Row. The distance was too great to pick out No. 2, but Annie May saw it in her mind as if she were a girl again.

Annie May Chappell was old even when she was a child because at eleven she became mother to Leanna, Ike, Martha Jane and George (the oldest). Her mother was dead at the age of thirty three, murdered by poverty, hardship and very regular pregnancy. Five living children there were and three others who had not survived her birth pangs. Leanna of the twinkling blue eyes had been the last to rest inside that tortured body and had only tasted the milk of a wet nurse and the care of her eldest sister.

The miner's cottage was second from the end of The Row. Whitewashed on the outside, with the front doorstep gleaming from the sandstone and elbow grease of three generations. Across the bailey was a steep sloping garden that yielded grudgingly, from its coal slag soil, a little supplement to the daily diet of the family. At the bottom, through a hole in the weary privet hedge was the river. A short path led from the hedge to a shallow river bed that provided generously the sandstone for the doorstep. Back up the hill of the garden stood the privy that from its lofty site viewed the majestic western hills of the valley, green in the daylight but a solid black when the sun said "Goodnight".

Inside the cottage was the living room filled with a sideboard, a horsehair sofa, a well scrubbed table with its family of four chairs. Dad's wooden armchair sat near the gleaming black-leaded range on which a black iron kettle sang all through the day after being filled from a cold water tap in the bosh near the door. There was a small side room, large enough to contain a round table covered with a deep scarlet cloth whose tassels reached the floor and provided a resting place for the family's only treasure - Dad's family bible.

A curved stone stairs led upwards from the door at the side of the fireplace to the two bedrooms - one of which led to the other. The smaller, inner room housed a double bed for the girls while the larger provided space for another double bed whose patchwork quilt kept Dad and George warm at the top and Ike, lying between their feet, at the other.

* * * * *

"George", Annie May's whispered shout reached up the short stone stairs. "It's half past five. You'll be late for work". On the side of the bed away from the wall, the sixteen year old George stirred, planted his feet on the rag mat at the side of the bed, dragged on his moleskin trousers, threw off his worn night-shirt and bare-footed and bare-chested made his way down the right hand side of the stairs to the bosh to splash himself ready for the day. While he pulled on the socks and boots, that Annie May warmed by the new born fire in the grate, he hastily scoffed the bread, cheese and onion she had prepared for him and downed Dad's mug that was filled with strong black tea. They didn't speak. It was far too early in the morning and George had four miles to walk to the Duffryn pit. He had no time to talk and anyway he didn't have anything to say. Breakfast done, he took his shirt from the brass rail above the fireplace, wrapped his muffler round his neck pulled on his cap and coat from behind the stairs door, took his box and jack off the table and with a goodbye grunt hurried off to catch up with Idris Howells who was already a hundred yards along the road to Duffryn.

Annie May closed the latch behind him. She poured herself a nice cup of tea and sat in Dad's chair for her first "ten minutes" of the day. She knew that Ike would rise soon. "Like the lark that he is", she said to one of the shapes among the now glowing coals on the fire. "Sings like one too - lovely boy".

This was her time of the day. Sitting alone thinking sometimes out loud, daydreaming, planning. Planning for them. George, he'd be on the coal face if he kept steady, regular in his attendance at the pit. Martha Jane was very good at school, especially at sums. She could get a job in a shop. In two years she would be leaving school. Then they would really be alright. George working and Martha Jane. Ike, oh, he'd be a great singer in the National Eisteddfod and a soloist in the Male Voice. Leanna - well she is so pretty, some rich man will snap her up and she will live in a big house and perhaps her husband would invite everyone to tea. "Don't be twp, she's only four".

And Dad. What a lovely man he used to be. "Like Peter in the Bible. The Rock". Short legged he was, with the small hips of a miner and a back and shoulders that could lift a dram half loaded with coal, and hands and arms that belonged to a blacksmith, but lifted you onto his shoulders with a tender strength that matched the music of his quiet Welsh bass. Oh Dad.

The first words of Annie May's favourite hymn invaded her line of thought as Isaac, whom everyone called Ike, announced that he was awake and everyone else should be too. Annie May loved to hear the sweetness of his voice but because she did not want it accompanied, at that time in the morning, with Leanna's demand for breakfast or Martha Jane's recitation of the times table (she could already recite them all up to eleven times and twelve times was her goal).

"Ike, do you know the time of day? Be quiet", silenced him at least until after Annie May had made sure he had "washed behind your ears" and he had crossed the bailey where he converted the privy into a concert hall. Then she stood at the door and dreamed like Ike, as his sweet soprano transported them both to a world that neither really understood. Concert over, Ike returned to eat his porridge with Martha Jane.

It was not a quiet time preparing those two for school but an observer would have felt, underneath the teasing, the noise and Annie May's sharpness, a close bond that tied them tightly together. They were a family - all six of them.

"Off you go kids. Mustn't be late for school", Annie May kissed them both. Martha Jane clung a little. Ike wiped the kiss off with frantic hands and Annie May propped the door open with the black leaded pebble she had brought back from the river once when she was searching for sandstone. Now it shone like ebony and adorned the step like a jewel.

Dressing Leanna was a joy. Her ready chuckle, rich blonde tresses and round blue eyes reminded Annie May of a doll she had seen once in the town, when the mine owner's wife and daughter rode by in their smart carriage.

"Go out and play on the bailey love", Annie May

prompted Leanna. "I think I can hear Sophie and May from next door".

Left alone in the living room, Annie May washed the few crocks that the others had used for breakfast and then made a bowl of porridge, using the only milk and sugar left until Friday. She opened the stairs door and moved purposefully to the first bedroom.

"Hallo Dad", she said quietly to the shape which faced the wall. "Have some breakfast love". The reply was no more than a scrape at the back of the man's throat and when Annie May gently turned him and propped him a little higher against the pillow, the dark, deep set eyes showed that George Chappell Senior was not living in this world. Something had gone from him. He was empty and had been so ever since Leanna had been born.

Annie May fed him the porridge and wiped his chin when he spilled some onto the quilt. She touched the bearded face and searched those vacant eyes for a glimpse of the one who had been The Rock.

Once downstairs, with Dad safely sat in his chair, Annie May polished and scrubbed and washed and mended and not until the church clock struck twelve did she have her second "ten minutes" of the day. She shared the pot of strong black tea with Dad and talked to him of the better times to come. Dad did not contradict her. Instead he sat and lived in his own place far away. "Say hallo to Mam", said Annie May over her shoulder as she washed the cups in the bosh.

A bacon hock from Lloyd's the Butchers and potatoes and root vegetables from the garden took little preparing in the afternoon for the family meal, and after George's wash down in the tin bath by the fire, they sat together round the table. Dad's armchair drawn to its proper place at the head of the table with Annie May, with Leanna at her knee, next to him on the right, so that she could take it in turns to help her small sister, lift the spoon of broth to Dad's mouth and find a little time to take her only nourishment of the day, if you did not count the tea during her "ten minutes". Martha Jane, Ike and George took the other chairs and the day's events were shared.

Martha Jane had nearly got her twelve times right and only Dai Jenkins, the doctor's son, was better than her. Ike had been chosen to sing solo in the Christmas concert and George - well George - concentrated on his broth. After all, he was a working man and did not have to bother himself with kid's talk.

When Annie May had washed the dishes and they were replaced in the side board, the heavy curtain pulled across the door, chairs pulled nearer the fire, Martha Jane - the scholar - opened the black bound bible at the next page. The nightly ritual would take them right through the "Good Book" and Martha Jane had taken over naturally when Dad had had to give up. She read well and nobody knew when biblical names did not quite correspond to the original. Hymns learned at the Rehobeth Methodist Chapel invariably followed and always ended with "Rock of Ages". These were precious times for the Chappells. "They were together and that was enough", thought Annie May but she knew as she looked across at the fine old armchair, that had belonged to the grandfather she had never known, with its listless passenger that they were not truly together and that The Rock needed to go to his resting place where his sweet gentle Elizabeth was surely waiting.

The younger ones and Dad had gone to bed. George, sensing something in Annie May that rarely surfaced, touched her hand that was cutting the bread and jam for his next day's box and with that touch spoke more eloquently than if he'd made a speech. "Night bach", replied Annie May.

Box finished, chairs returned to their table, door bolted, Bible marked and closed, tassels straightened, hearth brushed and tidied, oil lamp extinguished, Annie May - without the aid of a candle - climbed the cold stone stairs, passed the bed that housed the two men and Ike, reached for the latch of the second bedroom door, settled herself on the nearside of the bed and slept until five minutes later Leanna's dreaming called her and she took the tot lovingly to her bosom and whispered, "Sleep lovely, you've had a busy day".

CHAPTER TWO

Christmas that year, 1906, saw Ike take the first steps towards Annie May's fire light dreams for him. His solo at the school and a repeat performance in the chapel service, that marked the birthday of God's son, that the whole family attended - was acclaimed by all, including the Minister and Edwin Nicholls the choir's conductor and already Annie May's vision took her younger brother onto the platforms of all the chapels in all the towns she had ever heard of and beyond, to places she could not even name.

Two events in the new year made a difference. Young George had gone to work and the dregs of her morning tea had lost their heat and lay used and limp in the bottom of Annie May's cup when Ike stepped through the stairs door. Annie May had been so lost in her shapes and caverns and cliffs and private places ever changing in the early firelight that she did not see him even when he passed by to the bosh by the door. It was the running of the water tap that made her turn her head in surprise as her brother readied himself for school. "Cat got your tongue Ike?" she scolded. Ike's face was buried in the rough towelling and he gave her no reply. Instead he dropped the cloth, opened the door and crossed to his private place across the bailey, at the top of the garden.

Annie May's eyes followed him through the walls and a mother's concern hollowed her insides. "Was Ike not well? There was a fever in the next town". At the door now Annie May stood statue still. "What else could it be?" Then she knew. Ike was not singing. Those lovely tones, that filled her and all who heard them with the choruses of all the world's birds, were silent.

Ages passed and Ike, tear stained and gloomy ran across to Annie May's open arms and his plaintive "Oh, Annie May" sounded in a key that would move him much nearer manhood and off the platforms that Annie May's morning reveries had destined him.

The family gathered round. They helped Ike get over his

loss and never watched him when he soundlessly mouthed the words of the hymns in their evening gathering. It was Martha Jane who suggested that he should share the readings and it was not until St. David's Day that his loss again touched him deeply when Elsie James took his place in the school celebration. He did notice though how dark her eyes were and how the pulse at his temple quickened as she passed him on her return to her desk just across the aisle.

At home, month followed month with only the imperceptible changes of growing up. The pattern of the weeks was very much the same for Annie May and her trip down to the river, to renew her piece of sandstone, was an event. The hole in the hedge had closed somewhat with summer growth and Annie May could not easily get through. The bank was dry and the river bed exposed by six weeks of dehydrating sunshine.

A suitable stone rested at the near bank and took but a moment to yield itself to Annie May's grasp. She sat there as alone as at her morning "break" and allowed herself a holiday. Northward a small bridge escorted a cart across the stream and to her left about half a mile away nestled Pontygof school where Martha Jane had long since passed her twelve times table and Ike struggled with his nine times. The opposite bank was clothed in Summer dress and Annie May's thought was to take a little of its colour back to the cottage. The exposed stones were convenient steps and she felt coltish as she hopped to the opposite side. The daisies and yellow buttercups made a pathetic bouquet but to Annie May's mind they would clothe the home and "Not even Solomon in all his glory was arrayed like one of these".

It was with these thoughts she began her return crossing and perhaps it was because of her thoughts that she was almost unaware that the rain starved bank gave way under her lace-booted foot and that her head was received by the brutal edge of a rock riding high above the trickling water.

She knew not how long she lay there nor that George and Ike had found her and brought her to the cottage and laid her on the sofa. Mrs. Sarah Price had been sent for and, because she knew about such things, washed the nasty cut behind Annie May's left ear and explained, "She'll have a bit of a headache but there's nothing to worry about". Sure enough, Annie May felt better after a night's sleep and would have risen at five to get George off to work save that Martha Jane had taken over at least for the day and her, "You're to have a proper rest", was the signal for Annie May's first "proper rest" since her Mam had died five years before.

The next day arrived and life in the Chappell household returned to normal. The chores had been to seen to inside the house, in the garden and in the shop with its scant store of provisions and its ever increasing prices that left next to nothing, from the few shillings that George's sixty hours of labour earned, in the small leather purse that had belonged to Annie May's mother.

Yet Annie May never thought to complain of her life's lot. Her joy was in her family and it was only Dad's life-less life that caused her pain - but it was for him she hurt and knew that there was only one place where he would be alive again. Sometimes in her rare private moments, a cup of tea in her hand, she did sinfully wish him passed over. "Oh Dad".

Martha Jane and Ike had reached the Book of Ecclesiastes in their evening readings and Annie May "saw" that there was a time for this and a time for that, but she did not hear the words clearly. She only "saw".

Deafness, if only partial, is a handicap not to be welcomed but Annie May simply got on "cos things don't do themselves, do they?" George had to be got off to work Martha Jane and Ike had to be readied for school. Dad needed her attention and the household maintained. Leanna had to be seen to and entertained throughout the day. Annie May coped with it all and held the family together. But even she could not avert the inevitable.

She was the last to bed as she tended to the last chores of the day and then candleless she passed through the first bedroom with her right ear directed at the usual sounds of George's snores, Ike's teenage outcries and Dad's noises.

That night, an element was missing and even though

Annie May undressed in the inner bedroom and lay down beside Leanna, whose dreams that night needed no comforting, she knew what the morrow would bring.

"George Charles Chappell had been a pillar of the town", eulogised the Revd. Llewellyn. "A rich vein of coal he was. He will be sadly missed".

To Annie May's thinking, God had answered her unspoken prayer and she knew that Mam and Dad were entwined for all time.

Martha Jane was due to leave school and Annie May approached Tom Lloyd, the butcher, to procure a place for her sister in his employ. She was successful in this. At the end of the school year, Martha Jane was employed at Thomas Lloyd and Sons, Purveyors of Quality Meat - as a sweeper in the shop and meat store. "Still", thought Annie May, "it's a beginning".

George, the quiet one, the man, the provider, was closest to Annie May. They seldom had a conversation that lasted more than two minutes but their communication was absolute.

Three years after Dad's passing, their partnership was dissolved. George had called at the King's Arms for a well deserved pint of the best. In the bustle and the banter of the Public Bar, George sought a corner of the trestle where he could isolate himself and think his own thoughts. He shifted himself only once to refill his pot for his second drink and except for a nod or two to some of the men of The Row, he remained in his corner and never again moved. Something happened inside his head they were told.

Annie May buried her beloved brother next to her beloved Mam and Dad.

Annie May would not go to the parish for help. Martha Jane brought in a small amount and Ike, having left school began a career that lasted forty three years in the Post Office but George the man had gone and they - the family - had to survive.

Mrs. Eugene Cross needed a domestic. Mrs. Cross needed a skivvy and Annie May fitted the bill. She saw to the household and sent Ike and Martha to work and Leanna to school and still arrived at eight fifteen to clean Mrs. Cross' house, to wash and iron the dirty laundry, to prepare the vegetables and run the errands and bow to that pampered lady's every whim. She did not complain. Things were simply the way they were and her family had to eat. If she collapsed into bed at the end of the day she never counted the cost. She simply loved them and gave all that she had to give.

Ike, now welcomed in Elsie's home, sat at her family piano and saw, as Annie May had seen, a musical future. At first he only touched the keys and he dreamed, as his eldest sister had dreamed. The instrument would be his voice. But how?

Edwin Nicholls furnished the answer. That old man who had conducted and produced music for more than fifty years offered his services as a piano tutor and he had his reward, for in future years Ike wore a musical cap and gown and Elsie shared in his success.

Annie May stared into the fire and wondered at its mystic powers.

Only Leanna remained. But her early beauty was now surpassed and she broke many a heart, although she herself was never coquettish or even aware that she was truly lovely. She walked along the river bank under Annie May's watchful eye with many a beau until one summer's day, Owen Davies, the Removers - they owned two covered vans, horse drawn, and hired out when families changed houses, a fairly rare occurrence in those days - took her by the hand and she knew. Owen would be her life, would be her betrothed would be her only love.

* * * * *

So in 1914 Annie May found herself alone. Dad and George passed on. Ike in the Post Office - doing well - and dedicated to his piano and Elsie. Martha Jane still employed by Thomas Lloyd, etc., but aware of women's aspirations as equal citizens in tomorrow's world and Leanna living in with Mr. and Mrs. Davies, the Removers, with a plan to marry

Owen as soon as the law allowed. All this she remembered on Domen Fawr until the church clock struck and Annie May was surprised to count six chimes that collected her from her dreaming. She hoped going down the mountain would be easier than the climb had been.

She had no need to rush back but she knew that Mrs. Meyrick always worried if Annie May was out too long. Sure enough the kindly lady, small, grey haired and a little plump was leaning on the cast iron gate that opened onto a short stepped path that led into Gibbon's Villa, with its four bedrooms and a basement - converted for Annie May's use - and a double bayed front that lended the house a certain grandeur.

As Annie May approached, the Council's Senior Clerk came down the path and put his arm caringly around the shoulder of his wife and greeted the mountaineer with, "Got to the top did you? Lovely up there isn't it? Used to do it myself quite a bit when I was your age".

"None of your stories now" his wife gently chided.

"Come into the parlour Annie May. We'll have a cup of tea". She followed them inside and as the door closed behind them Annie May had a feeling of being home again when Mam and Dad had been there.

In the Villa that had been her home since her brothers and sisters had made their own way - since she was alone - she applied herself to her new way of life.

Annie May was paid three shillings a week and found, for which she maintained the domestic and cooking needs - although Mrs. Meyrick loved to help out in preparation for the day's main meal - and tended to the needs of the three young children. The girls were aged six and seven and the eldest, a son, was eleven.

Her nature would not but allow her to love her new charges - her new family.

Dorithea was the youngest. A blonde haired cherub in the mould of Leanna and her equanimity needed no coercion or even correction. If a better behaved, more balanced child existed in the world, Annie May had yet to see it. She tended all the needs of this little tot - she washed and dressed and fed and satisfied the little child on every front and enjoyed the tiny fingers squeezed around her neck for a goodnight kiss and saw her off - sound asleep.

Margaret was different from her sister. Taller, darker - on her father's side - and perhaps, because of a year's extra maturity, a little more forceful. "I'm going to be a, something", she often said and Annie May knew that one day this embryo would take charge of some part of the world in which they lived, perhaps never to rule but, to have a contribution to make.

Clarence was her chief problem. Eleven years old. Intelligent, sensitive and manipulative. At tea and the evening visits of Mr. and Mrs. Meyrick the boy was all virtue. His parents - lovely folk - saw the charm of their son and often presented him to their visitors and Mr. Meyrick's colleagues as "Our ideal son" who would mature to take a leading role in the town and country and "who knows?" beyond.

The boy made frequent visits to the town and responded to Annie May's questions with "I've been with the boys". He prospered at his lessons and the local headmaster proclaimed him the highest achieving pupil of the year and it was certain, that a young star was being nurtured in that deprived community to lead the future generation into a new and better world.

Every Saturday morning a little ceremony was performed. It was pay day and Mr. Meyrick's profession, a little pomposity and a sense of the Victorian prompted him to line up his family and servant so that he could preside over and present their weekly allowance. Mrs. Meyrick received first a sum always hidden from sight and further concealed as Mr. Meyrick closed Mrs. Meyrick's fingers over the coins.

Clarence received, with a directive to be prudent, a penny ha'penny and the girls a penny each. Annie May received hers last. Her place and her wages befitting a servant. She knew her place and accepted who she was and where she belonged.

Invariably Saturday afternoon meant a trip with the girls to spend their weekly wealth. All the delights of The

Chocolate Lady's Shop awaited the tiny company and scanning the window, full of bull's-eyes and gobstoppers and Five Boy's chocolates, was part of the adventure for Annie May and the two youngest members of the Meyrick household. Their pennies were soon spent and their return to the Villa was filled with the satisfied cries and chocolate smeared faces of two little girls and the content filled heart of their guardian, one Annie May.

Clarence was allowed to go alone "up to town" as befitted his almost twelve years and he always returned at the appointed hour and replied to the oft repeated question "With the boys".

Annie May put her wages in a tin on the mantelpiece of her basement room and, when required, spent a shilling here and a sixpence there. She never made a note of her store of wealth. Whit Sunday was upon them and she decided to "rig herself out" and of a Saturday evening she tipped up the tin and discovered 17s 6d. The amount surprised her. She had "spent up" for Christmas but apart from the purchase of a pair of boots and her weekly contribution of three pence in the Sunday collection she had spent nothing. Surely she should have in excess of £1.10s. 0d. in her tin!

She decided to tell Mr. Meyrick of her loss and then immediately changed her mind. She did not want suspicion to rest upon the household. Perhaps she had forgotten some significant purchase.

It was not until washing day later that she shook Clarence's play trousers, while he was in school, to prepare them for the Monday tub, scrubbing board and mangle, that a half crown coin, a florin, a silver threepenny piece and some coppers scattered onto the oilclothed floor of the boy's bedroom. She collected them on hands and knees with a numbed heart. A total of five shillings and tuppence ha'penny.

Her mind knew, her heart hoped. He was a small boy in a small inescapable realm. If she "clecked" to his dad, he would forever be blackened as a thief. If she said nothing and did nothing, she would condemn the boy to days of anguish and loneliness. Annie May had been there.

She took the money, put it in her purse and arranged the day so that she could meet Clarence at the school gates.

He ran with his friends, unaware of the moment. Annie May stopped him in full flight and invited him to walk home with her. The event was so unusual that Clarence was at once bemused, startled and apprehensive.

Enough to say that by the time that they had reached the little bridge that led to the Villa, Annie May's buying power had increased by four shillings. Clarence had a little more than a shilling, that bought a life long philosophy. To his credit, he never betrayed it and entered, a long time on, as Treasurer to the local council.

The Meyrick's household nurtured that simple soul. The psychology of all that passed she could not understand nor articulate. But everything that she experienced impinged upon her thinking and led her on to some distant goal that was in her mind. Where it was or when it would be she could not know but she knew that there was something that she did not know and, "one day will be".

The hills were her escape. Nothing intruded when she was in the hills, though she never again attempted the arduous climb up Domond Fawr. Other lesser mounds attracted and entranced her and on work days, at the washing line or the ragging of a window pane, her eyes scanned the parapets of her valley that guarded her and gave her security - but oddly enough provided a kind of yearning too.

CHAPTER THREE

Early lunch on Sundays meant the rest of the day off. Annie May had never had a day off before, if you did not count the time she had been ill. Sunday afternoons. Time to herself, time to visit the cemetery and pay tribute to those dear ones gone on, and on beyond the cemetery - the hills; those steep walls that hemmed the valley in, along whose narrow channel ran the river, that once had trapped her and created the habit of carrying her head a little to the left "to give her right ear a chance?" Where does it come from, this silvery snake?" she often asked the hills out loud and one Sunday she searched the source. Six miles to the north she found the hillside trickle, or rather there were three of them and she named their confluence "Trinity" for it seemed to her a place where God dwelt.

Among the hills Annie May felt what she could not understand. At their ridges she could see to hills beyond and she knew there were other places to go. Not to travel to, not to leave her valley - no she did not want to leave. But there was more - she knew. She just knew.

Ike was going to leave, he said. Going to Australia he was one day with Elsie. Martha Jane travelled all the way to Newport one summer to talk about politics and Leanna would move down the valley when she and Owen were married. No! Annie May did not want to move. She wanted to stay and learn of that which surrounded her. She had found Trinity - the beginning. "Where was the end?" Martha Jane said that the river ended in the Bristol Channel. But that was not what she had meant. She did not even know the questions to ask. How could she ever know the answer?

One Sunday, about eighteen months into her service with Mrs. Meyrick, Annie May had taken the girls to morning Sunday School and lunch had been cleared away. She sat at a sheltered spot on the eastern wall of the valley above The Row, a place she rarely returned to now that the family was "gone". She found in the black draw string bag, never left behind, a hymn book she had not returned to its proper place in the Chapel after the Sunday School service. Guilt and a little fear of Revd. Llewellyn, soon gave way to common sense. She would return the book next Sunday.

She opened the small coal black book and found number 498 - "Rock of Ages". The index in the back was of no use to Annie May. Alphabetical would have been a foreign concept to her untutored mind but she knew where her favourite hymns were. The Rock, of course, was easy, as was number 528 "In Heavenly Love Abiding", but as falteringly she read one more and another, the poets fanned in her the spark that was waiting to be ignited. That day she read thirty hymns and they did not deepen a sense of religion. She was not "saved" as the Revd. Llewellyn tried to frighten her to be. No! She was simply moved inside by a knowledge, an instinct, by an awareness of the future and the past, that defied all schooling, all rational thought. Annie May had a vision. A vision so simplistic.

To leave the valley was not a practicality, but to search for knowledge of the unknown was within the grasp of every educated person. She was not such a one and had no chance to be so. She could only pass on her insight to those that followed. This was Annie May's dream.

Life did not change much for this visionary. But on a particular Sunday, early evening, when she sat with the stolen hymn book in her lap and deepened her resolve, her dream, a shadow fell over the pages. It was a real shadow. It was the shadow of a soldier. One, Ifor Booth, recently recruited to the South Wales Borderers in order to win the Great War across the sea. He was nineteen years old, lived in the middle of the town with his Mam and his Dad who was a miner and a soloist in the Male Voice.

"Sorry if I disturbed you", he said. "Just wondered what a lovely girl like you was doing by yourself".

Lovely girl", she thought "Who ever said I was lovely? I'm only reading my old hymn book", said Annie May.

"I've got a favourite" proclaimed Ifor. "Number 620. Do you like that one too?"

She turned the pages and arrived at "Who Would True Valour See?"

Ifor was certainly handsome. Blonde - not dark and Welsh like. Tall - not short and Welsh like. Slim - not Welsh like at all!

He was not like the others either and he did not find it necessary to drink himself into a quarrel on a Saturday night at the King's Arms or The Drysiog.

Ifor had passed the scholarship and had been to the County School and he was certainly attractive to the repressed sexuality of Annie May. He sought her out - mostly on Sunday, her day off - but sometimes, when the Brecon Barracks allowed him home, on work days when she brought the children home from school or when she pegged the washing on the line or sometimes when she saw him through the Villa's window and could not speak.

Mrs. Meyrick was nobody's fool and was a very kindly soul and she missed little that passed between the lovers. "Annie May", she said one auspicious day. "Why don't you invite your young man home to tea?"

And so she did. Sunday it was. When else? There was salad and cold meat and jelly and custard. Annie May had done them all proud and after tea Mr. and Mrs. Meyrick and all the little Meyrick's went for a walk in the park to listen to the town band playing.

Ifor and Annie were left alone in the parlour. I do not know what passed between them but three months later they married. Mr. and Mrs. Booth senior attended the wedding but when Ifor embarked for France, Annie May was alone again, a servant of the kindly Mr. and Mrs. Meyrick in the Villa where young love had ripened and in total propriety had been fulfilled.

Letters received were few and far between. In any case Annie May had to recruit Martha Jane - now married to a local councillor - to transcribe her message of love for the future and a speedy end to this blasphemy called "The fight for King and Country". "The War to end all Wars". Ifor wrote of hope that he would soon be home. He omitted the carnage, the blood and guts, the futility of it all. He only said that he loved her and the child that she was carrying. His hope was for a boy but a girl would be alright.

Annie May's son would be a scholar. Ifor and she and their son would live to see better times. Education was the key. Education that was beyond schooling; moral values, worthiness, excellence and above all a caring that she would never in the whole of her life expect for herself but only for her family. All these things she would pass on through her son.

In its season, the child was born. She was named Ruth and Annie May could see in her, in her cornflower eyes, in her halo of almost white hair and the long tapering fingers - so unlike her own work worn stumps - in her long limbs a replica of Ifor. Ruth flourished and the neighbours said they had never seen a lovelier child. The first six weeks were a delight for Annie May. She nursed Ruth abundantly and observed her every stirring. She saw in her the third element of another Trinity. Each morning she thanked God for a new day to be spent caring for her little one and each Sunday she carried Ruth in the Welsh shawl that Mrs. Meyrick had given to her, up to visit Ifor's Mam and Dad and then on to show her to Grandma and Grandad Chappell and Uncle George.

On the morning of Ruth's sixth Sunday, she lay lifeless in her cot. Mrs. Price - who knew about such things - said some word to explain it. Annie May did not hear.

CHAPTER FOUR

Annie May nursed her grief. She shared it with no-one not even Ifor, although, of course, she did write to tell him - "Somewhere in France".

Her solace was in recalling all the moments she and Ifor had shared.

"I wondered what a lovely girl like you was doing by yourself" had been their introduction on the hillside as she read her "old hymn book".

Ifor had read it with her and because he had been to the County School the words had sounded even better and more lovely. He had walked beside her down to the town that day and the two miles had seemed too little distance to her, but at the bridge that led to the Villa they had said "Solong" and gone their ways but she had taken a backward glance and watched for a second or two that straight, strong back, swinging arms and golden head as they retreated towards the town. "He's nice", she said to herself and it was only when the passing Rita Edwards who lived next door turned her head that Annie May realised that she had spoken out loud.

As she pegged Mr. Meyrick's shirts onto the wire washing line a peaked cap followed by two dancing eyes peeped over the wall at the back of the Villa and Annie May's heart missed a beat. She had been startled to be sure and she had turned to see if anyone were watching but the missed heart beat had sprung from another source. Familiar to Annie May but different. They met the following Sunday, by appointment. "Three o'clock by Waun Pound pond" was how Ifor had actually invited her and in a rainstorm they walked together sharing the birth of the loveliest of human emotions.

There had only been ten meetings before Mrs. Meyrick's invitation to Sunday tea and nearly all were on the hillside. Once Annie May took Ifor to the river's source and he saw the joining of the streams as they fell down the hill. "Father, Son and Holy Ghost", he said and pointing with the rush whip they had plaited together he counted out loud "One two three".

That had been a blessed moment for Annie May for somehow they had made a lifetime's communication inside the limits of a phrase or two. She had been reminded too how George - the family's provider - had been able to talk with just a touch of his hand.

Whit Sunday had been a special day. The Sunday School anniversary was celebrated and for once the remaining family, Martha Jane, Ike, Leanna and Annie May had all been together for the evening service. Annie May's friend was a surprise but his natural good looks and above all his obvious devotion to their "mother" won them all, even Martha Jane - whose political pursuits prompted a distrust of men - although she advised her eldest sister that even Ifor was "the same as all the others".

Tea with the Meyrick's and afterwards in the parlour was a happening that returned to Annie May again and again as she saw it in her mind and in the reds and blacks and greys of the shifting coals spending their lives in the lonely firegrate in the basement of the Villa. The days and weeks that followed scrambled themselves into a stew. Marriage, mending, washing, waiting, missing periods, letters, cleaning, hoping, no news, war, victories, losses. "Oh the losses", Ike's piano exams, Martha Jane's votes, Leanna's blue eyes and Ruth's and the photograph. Ifor had had it taken in Brecon. Smart he was in his uniform there on the mantelpiece between the pair of gleaming brass candlesticks (a present from Ifor's Mam and Dad) and the china dogs with their golden chains that guarded her most precious possession. Ifor had given it to her as he boarded the London Midland Scottish railway carriage so long ago as he went to do his bit. He had looked back until the train had turned the bend and Annie May had stayed for a long time, still seeing his fine features and communicating her love to each passing cloud that chased the chariot of war down the valley to the port, and on to heartbreak.

Of course, she worked. What else did she know? But what would be the outcome? Ifor's return was the catalyst to the future, the better times for all. When this Great War was finished the world would be alive and ready for the future.

Yet it continued and Annie May's life remained as it had always been - work and dreams. She dreamt of things past but the fire in the hearth yielded not its secrets of the future and so she simply bore her grief for Ruth and her longing for Ifor's return and "got on with it".

CHAPTER FIVE

The eleventh day of the eleventh month dawned and bells rang through the town. The school children were given a day's holiday and chapels and churches overflowed. Mothers, Grandmothers, wives and sweethearts wept openly and even some of the men suddenly caught sniffling colds. Annie May went to tea with the Meyricks and had a lovely time and then she waited to hear when Ifor would return. She knew that France was a long way and that she should be patient but when the New Year bells had rung, with no word, she went to see Ike who used his influence in the Post Office to ask the supervisor to ask the Post Master if he could make some enquiries. She visited Martha Jane to see if Councillor Evans could find out what was happening.

The very next day she knew - by official letter. Lance Corporal Ifor Rhys Booth would arrive at Newport Station by troop train on 7th January 1919 at 1.30 p.m.

Less than a week and they would be together again and they would put the "old war" behind them. She must do something about their home. Spotless thought it already was, she polished and rubbed and scrubbed and spent extra minutes on that old armchair that had for so long nestled her father and would now hold her husband home safe.

On the 5th of January, Annie May made a decision. She would go to Newport to meet Ifor. Exactly where it was she did not know and it would be at least twenty miles further than she had ever travelled before. In fact, it would be the only occasion that she had left the town but go she would to bring back her Ifor. Martha Jane offered to go with her but had to be content with seeing her off at the station on the 10.45 a.m. and advising her eldest sister about waiting on Platform 2 to meet the train from Paddington. As Annie May said to her, "This trip is for me and Ifor".

The two carriage train in its red and gold trim livery busily threaded its way southward. The pit head at Duffryn, black against the valley's walls passed on the right hand side and Annie May, alone in the compartment, remembered her brother and her dad. Then on she flew to new towns and villages - strangely alike with their ribbons of cottages lined up in terraces along the contours of the valley. And always beside the railway, though sometimes on the left and sometimes on the right, ran the river. Annie May had seen its birthplace and now she was sharing its life as they travelled together to their journeys' end. The river to the sea and she to meet Ifor.

About thirty minutes into the journey, the train made its fifth stop and Annie May's thoughts were interrupted as the compartment's door opened and a young woman wrapped against the January air, tidied herself into the opposite corner. As the journey continued the two held no conversation but merely shared the space and dwelt inside their own heads.

Eight miles and three stops later, the scenes had changed. No longer were the hills in view and the river had disappeared along some hidden route, the cottages gave way to houses each big enough to shelter fifty people. Trains passed on either side as Newport Station swallowed up Annie May's carriage. The young woman alighted first and Annie May almost bumped into her as she turned and asked, "Do you know where the train from London is?"

Winnie Rees was going to meet her brother who was coming home from the war. He had been away for more than two years and mother was not well enough to make the journey.

The two crossed the bridge to Platform 2 and by the huge clock they could see that the London train was still an hour away.

"Why don't we get a nice cup of tea?" asked Winnie. "In the BuffET".

"That's a funny word", thought Annie May thinking they would be banged about. That day the caterers did a roaring trade, for hundreds made their way to Newport Railway Station - grandads and grandmothers, brothers, sisters, wives, uncles, aunts, friends, fathers, mothers, boys and girls and babes in arms. This was the day the war would end for them

- the day their dear ones would be home. The Buffet lived up to its reputation and Annie May and her new friend had to stand, hemmed against a man of large proportions, his equally obese wife and the wall by the arched window, hardly able to lift the thick mugs of stale brew to drink.

The train at long last announced itself with a throaty belch and a sibilance that was lost in the cheers and rowdiness and the joy and the hope shared by every soul on Platform 2. It came into view bearing the crossed flags of Regiment and Union and at every opened window eager faces and searching eyes viewed the platform for someone familiar that would signal his home coming.

Annie May lost her new friend in the very first moment of the surging of the crowd and a little later caught only a frozen image of Winnie with her arms around her brother, who walked with the aid of a T crutch as he dragged his right foot towards the platform's exit.

"Wounded", said Annie May in a whisper. "Please God let Ifor not be wounded", she mouthed.

Ifor had not been hit by shot nor shell and as he alighted from the train Annie May's heart touched her eyes and through her tears and the crowd - now somewhat thinned, for Ifor's had been the last carriage - she forced herself towards him. She wrapped herself around him unashamed and loved him welcome home. They spoke not at all and it was not until they sat in the compartment of the valley train that Annie May saw how tired he was, the weight he had lost, the two deep vertical lines permanently sculpted in a frown between his lovely blue eyes that seemed, even as he viewed the valley for recognised landmarks, to be looking elsewhere, perhaps to the place he had come from, "over there".

"It's alright love", Annie May soothed. "We'll soon have you right - at home again".

But she was wrong!

Mam and Dad Booth invited all the family to a 'Welcome Home' for Ifor. The town council put on a special event on the Recreation ground at Easter for all the returned heroes. A fund was set up to build a memorial to the Glorious Dead -

more than twenty from that small town. Annie May attended all the functions and took Ifor along with her. He hardly knew where he was. Day followed day, never changing. Annie May still tended to the needs of the Meyrick household, keeping the basement like a new pin and trying to love Ifor back to the life that those years on a foreign field had shell shocked him away from.

"How's Ifor?", enquired the happy-go-lucky voice of Amos Reed who lived in No. 5. "D'you think he's up to having half a pint down the King?"

Annie May could not remember Ifor's ever having been in a public house and her "No thanks" to Amos was instinctive, but as he turned away she clutched at something new. Perhaps men's company, men's talk would stir Ifor into the present and lead him through the shadow that troubled him and bring him 'home again'.

"Amos", she called. "I'll see if Ifor wants to go".

Ifor was taken down to the pub that day and, in the weeks that followed, the short passage from the Villa to the Kings Arms became a daily journey for the tormented man; soon, with or without Amos. His usual drink was drawn ready from the cask by landlord Ted as Ifor passed the 'Snug' and proceeded to the public bar.

The corner of the trestle - the same one that George had sat on - became Ifor's place. Rarely did he extend his order beyond three halves and Annie May resisted the new minister's pressure at the chapel to make Ifor 'go Temperance' for he was calmed by his daily tipple it seemed.

Day by day reality grasped at his mind but night time sent him once more into those muddy places where noise and disorder and meaninglessness and despair blocked his progress.

Annie May loved him more and more and in those afternoon hours when Ifor was down at the Kings Arms, she prayed standing up at the bosh or on her knees, beside their bed or going to the shops or when she escorted the children, or when she went to chapel and most of all when she searched in the firelight that had ever been her inspiration. The night hours passed, prompted by sudden shouts and sobbing from the young man reliving those hours and days and months and torments in another place. Annie May did not know what to do. Her night times found her wide awake, endlessly seeking solutions to the problems of the dear one who lay beside her. His outbursts were frequent and sometimes punctuated by wanderings around their one roomed home and then his return to the bed signalled a few hours of exhausted sleep for Annie May.

Awakening from such a sleep, when the first shafts of dawn were creeping in through the curtains at the basement window, she reached for Ifor and found him gone. Immediately awake, her eyes peered through the early gloom and rested on Ifor's shape, strangely hunched over the earthenware sink in the far corner.

"Ifor love" she soothed as she stretched for him, vaguely aware that the tap was running and she was rewarded as Ifor's right hand swung backwards as if to ward off some unseen foe. The keen edge of the razor gouged deeply into the mastoid bone behind Annie May's right ear and trailed towards her windpipe. The shock of it felled her and it was Mrs. Meyrick - on a rare visit to the basement - who found them. Annie May was moaning and the congealed blood at her throat told the story in part, as did the dreadful gash on Ifor's left wrist and the forever closed eyes of a haunted young man.

* * * * *

There were three ceremonies performed ten days later. The first, at the green draped graveside where stood some dozen black clad men. Among them were the Reverend Pearce with his "Ashes to ashes and hope of resurrection", Ike whose thoughts were with Annie May, unforgiving of his dead brother-in-law, Cyril Evans, one hand holding his bowler hat across his best and his other in the left hand pocket of his long black coat, thumb protruding in a proper councillor like stance, Owen Davies who had arranged the funeral because of his connections in the transport business and Amos who was dying for a pint and Edward Booth, bowed and tearful as he saw his only son lowered into the uncaring clay.

At the house, the women, led by Martha Jane and Leanna, saw to the ceremony of the funeral feast. Ham and tongue and boiled potatoes were served.

Annie May - bandage partly hidden under a black draped hat and a high collared dress - sat on the chair, far away from the sink in the corner. Elsie stood beside her and told her that things would be alright.

The men returned and sat at the table to enjoy the fine fare made even tastier by several dishes of varied pickles.

But as one o'clock struck by Christchurch clock the crown began to drift away. The first to leave was Cyril Evans who had to be away on council business. An hour later Annie May had only Martha Jane and Leanna to help her through the day.

Cyril Evans was at the forefront of the day's third ceremony, for in the middle of the town, the Chairman of the Council unveiled a statue depicting three men in battle dress. Underneath in finely carved capitals, were the names of the men who had given their lives in the Great War 1914-1918.

The name Ifor Rhys Booth was not included.

* * * * *

That night Leanna stayed with her eldest sister and slept beside her as she had done when the family had lived in The Row. She witnessed tears and sobbing out loud that she had never seen before and as she cradled that anguished head, her fingers gently smoothed the bandage behind Annie May's right ear.

* * * * *

Leanna and Martha Jane and Elsie gave as much of themselves as they could afford, to Annie May's adjustment. That their own lives and problems intervened was no criticism of them. Ike organised. But in the end, Annie May was left alone. She dealt with the responsibilities of her employment, although the Meyrick family asked for nothing and even employed a young girl to help her out until she re-established herself.

It was the basement itself that prevented her from returning to the way it was. The bed was Ifor's bed. The wooden chair was Ifor's chair. The mirror at which he shaved was placed above the bosh and that was the place she never wanted to return to. Annie May lived those months in a kind of limbo. Of course, she carried on to the world as if nothing had happened and invitations to tea and chapel were often and regular. She accepted too. Everyone made her welcome and at a particular social when the "Plate was spun" and David Ellis chose her, in the military two step and she saw that he wore the same insignia that another had worn, a peace enveloped her and normality almost returned.

David did not understand. How could he? He had not been to the war but only to training camp and at the end demobilisation had left him pretending to have been a soldier.

He escorted Annie May to her basement step and seemed to be Ifor until he tried to kiss her. "Don't" she said. "Go home David. You don't understand".

Then one evening, the day almost done, she sat beside the dying embers of the fire's feeble blaze and the future was revealed.

The carbon curtain shifted and she saw the valley, stark and real and a slash of charcoal, that took her from where she was into another place.

"Sorry if I disturbed you", his voice said. "Lovely girl", he had called her.

Annie May shut her eyes and sang in a sweet quiet voice, "Who would true valour see, let him come hither".

"He had been valiant" she thought - "out there in that Godforsaken mud".

But on the hillside before those dreadful days, he had been blonde and handsome and straight and slim and tall.

His visits had been few - determined by the whim of a bullying uncouth sergeant in the barracks at Brecon.

"Got a bit of stuff 'av yer? Stick it in fer me".

Ifor was gentle and their walks and their talks flourished into pure innocent 1916 love. He asked her permission to hold her hand and dropped it quickly if a fellow traveller ventured near. They rejoiced in the hills and in the river and in poetry and in dreams - that were the same.

He returned her one Sunday evening, in the early dusk to the gates of the Meyrick's Villa and moved away but a step or two towards Brecon and his army life. Then he returned.

"I love you Annie May", he whispered. She did not hear but she knew what he said and her reply was lost in a gentle surrender of their lips that silently, delicately, irrevocably, joined them together.

She had her memories and if they hurt they also sustained her and though she would never forget her own true love she had to go on. "In another place" she thought.

* * * * *

"Why could she not go away?" was her crie de coeur.

CHAPTER SIX

The Reverend Pearce, a regular visitor to the distressed widow had a sister in the nearest valley and he was sure that a reliable, hardworking girl like Annie May would be more than welcome. So it was, although it took several weeks in the arranging, she left her home, sold her few possessions, she gave Grandad's chair to Leanna and taking with her no more than the old black leaded kettle, the polished sandstone, the brass candlesticks and her precious picture of her beloved Ifor, she emigrated to a foreign valley just five miles away.

Oddly, the Reverend Pearce's sister had married a Pearce, Minister of the local chapel and Annie May often confused the who with the what. But her straightforwardness and hard work soon won over both sides of the family and they knew that they had acquired a treasure.

She kept in touch with Ike and her sisters by walking - on a Sunday - to her homeland and on occasion one or more of her siblings ventured in the opposite direction.

Her responsibilities were minimal. She had only to clean the Pearce household, a three bedroomed, two reception dwelling. There were no children and her own attic abode was sparse and undemanding. There was time - a commodity undreamt of in Annie May's conscience - when she could pursue whatever she wanted to pursue.

Of course, that was a problem.

Where then was this near thirty year old to end up? This lady who had endured the death of half a dozen loved ones, who had nurtured her siblings into adulthood, who had known nothing but hardship and constant toil. What did the God above deem to be her future?

Life changed little for Annie May. She worked as hard as ever, was poorly paid although made happy and welcome by the Reverend and Mrs. Pearce. One thing had changed though but, because she was now among people who as yet did not know her well, no-one realised that she no longer presented her right ear to the sounds around her. That awful blade had cut deeply into the bone behind her right ear and reduced its function, and she soon learned that she could "hear" better if she read the words on people's lips. So it remained for the rest of her life. She was totally deaf in one ear because of the accidental blow of the river stone and partially deafened in the other by the events of the most terrible morning of her life.

In her moments of retrospection, she remembered over and over the blessed times - few though they had been - she had shared with Ifor and those six enchanted weeks when Ruth had been a joy. Not ever did she condemn God for his cruelty and it never entered her head to even consider that Ifor had struck her. Some inner demon bred in the mud, desolation and despair "over there" had struck. "Not you Ifor, my lovely" she whispered again and again.

Martha Jane visited sometimes and presented her views on the changing political scenario of the post war years. She also produced three sons and a daughter in due course.

Ike received his cap and gown for his L.R.A.M. and Annie May's heart burst with pride for her brother's achievement and she reflected on the hours she had spent searching the embers of The Row's firelight and she decided that the fire had spoken to her. Or perhaps it had been God. She was never sure which.

Leanna married well and was financially secure. She had married for love and that love was fulfilled when Owen and Leanna's son, Glyn, was the outcome of two people well met and well matched. Annie May was proud of them all.

* * * *

Set in a narrow spur leading to its parent valley, huddled together along a single road leading steeply downhill from the newly opened garage at the top - the community clung together in houses that boasted front rooms, to be used on Sundays only and could be proud also of a new school, built in 1912, the Inn directly opposite the chapel and the Manse erected in the same grounds.

It was the Primitive Methodist Chapel that proved a focal

point for Annie May. She discovered that she had a slight singing voice and joined the choir - actually able to hear quite well from inside the combined sound of forty voices. She never missed a meeting of the Sisterhood at seven o'clock on Thursday evenings and Sunday meant two attendances at the chapel at eleven a.m. and six o'clock sharp.

Annie May remained with the Reverend and Mrs. Pearce. They could not replace her industry, her loyalty, her faithfulness and she adjusted. If she did not actually put the dreadful happenings of the past completely out of her mind she knew that, "life goes on and I must get on with it".

She also had a new factor in her life. Time. Her duties no longer required eighteen hour days. She had time to explore. She searched these new hills in all the seasons' garbs and found a new special place called The Nook. Others knew of it too but Annie May thought of the little dingle as "Her Place". She discovered the Library three miles "down town" and, using Reverend Pearce's endorsement, became a joining member of the Miner's Welfare Hall and Institute.

"There aren't those many books in the world, she gaped. "Reverend Pearce has three shelves full, but this place has thousands - millions". That 'fact' she observed at her first visit, as she wandered aimlessly around the pillared edifice to knowledge and even onto the balcony, grandly presided over by a fine oil painting of the chairman of the Town Council sporting his chain of office. Not knowing her own literary needs she brightened at the section marked POETRY for the label prompted her and she remembered her joy of discovery on the hillside at home. "Was it nine years ago that Ifor had interrupted my faltering efforts to read from the black hymn book?"

'Classification' and 'alphabetical' still had no meaning so she chose two poetry books from a shelf set at eye level and did not notice the patronising sniff and raised eyebrows of the librarian as he officiously date stamped the books and placed the library cards into the filing system.

In her room, back at the Manse, she sat down on the old leather chair, brass studded, work worn and comforting - a throw out from the Reverend Pearce's study - and began to read by the flickering light of the gas mantle recently installed in all the rooms of the Manse.

With difficulty she read the title "Samson Agonistes" and expected to relive the life of the Bible Hero but ten lines into Milton's gem the metre and the words baffled Annie May. She turned the page and read the rhymes 'Saint' and 'faint' and 'grave' and 'gave' and 'right' and 'delight' in Milton's 'On his dead wife'. The title itself returned her mind to her lost love. "Who is Alcestis and Jove?" she asked the page. "This Milton is too hard for me". She turned to the second volume in despair but John Masefield's opening line from Cargoes "Quinquireme of Ninevah from distant Ophir. Rowing home to heaven....." added to the heaviness that lay upon her. She knew what ivory was and apes and peacocks but "Stately Spanish galleon coming from the Isthmus" closed the book for her.

She had known years before, that she was not destined to be educated and with the loss of Ruth and no hope of more children her dream was dead too.

In the silence of her room Annie May wept.

* * * * *

She retained the two unread volumes until the 'return date', which was stamped inside the covers, then made her way with disillusioned steps to the grand library building.

"I'll hand them in and say I'll call again", she decided in that half out loud voice typical of the hard of hearing and pushed the inner swing doors to face Miss Maggie Weed, who sat in the place of the other librarian who had seemed to be such an important gentleman.

"You're fond of poetry then?" asked the tall, almost gaunt Miss Weed.

"Well yes", blurted out the reply, "but these were too hard for me. You see I haven't read all that much at all".

Maggie was interested in all the library members' requirements. Five minutes of conversation told her much of

Annie May's background and limited reading skill and experience. She took her by the hand and led her to easier publications.

From that day, the assistant librarian became Annie May's guide through that sea of books and, because of her gentleness and patience, her profound joy in literature and an awareness of Annie May's needs, the latter explored the world of lesser poets and her proudest possession arrived in time for Christmas Day that year. It was "The Golden Treasury" and on the flyleaf, in beautiful copper plate, was the legend:

> 'To Annie May
> From your friend Maggie
> Christmas 1923 '

* * * * *

Annie May shared The Nook with Maggie and, the daughter of a collier met with the daughter of a pit manager and a bond was sealed that lasted until they passed on - sixty years in the future.

The Nook tucked itself away, close to the road, but some divine landscape architect had conceived its design. Not twenty paces from the entrance a stream babbled its way through ferns and the so green grasses, through the clay bound banks and on to where alders grew, where sunlight found itself dispensed into myriads of colours and created reflections and shadows that reached beyond into fantasy. Annie May was alive in The Nook and she brought to Maggie an extension to her library life. Maggie undoubtedly helped Annie May to reach forward, to confirm her belief in education. But Annie May, as ever, gave more than she received and Maggie learned from her tutor that, in this life, people mattered more than anything else and that a simple soul had much to say.

Many an hour they spent in that enchanted place and Annie May would ever claim to be the more blessed. "Maggie helped me with my education", she said. "I wish I could read better so she wouldn't have to work so hard with me".

In their leisure time they walked together and talked together and were silent together. It was to Maggie only that Annie May spoke of her loss at the parting of her loved ones; Mam, Dad, George, Ruth and Ifor and Maggie returned the compliment.

Her well to do family had sent her to a convent school in England and the cloistered, ordered, scholastic atmosphere had well suited the organised, academic mind that accompanied her tall slim frame and too long features. University followed and second class honours degree. She applied for and succeeded in obtaining an assistant teacher's post in a girl's school in Cardiff, where she enjoyed her work and began her life outside in the world. She met Clifford Morris.

Clifford was a clerk in a shipping office and, to Maggie's inexperienced mind, sophisticated and worldly wise and when, one evening he said, "You would if you loved me" she knew not how to say "No".

But it was no act of love and the callous, brutal assault left Maggie bleeding, bruised and humiliated. She never saw Clifford again. She left her post and returned to her home town and the library.

"I know you'll never tell a living soul", she said to Annie May.

Day by day their lives were no more than ordinary but a bond had been cemented and Maggie and Annie May were the most cherished of humans - they were true friends.

Sometimes in that cloistered community there were events. The chapel had its anniversary and the Sunday school. Processions through the village and on into the town meant weeks of rehearsal for Whit Sunday. Anthems were practised by the choir and the children were prepared and best suits and frocks were a symbol of belonging, certainly not of affluence since no-one - not even Cartwright the Shop - was affluent. No-one could be described as well off, unless you spoke in muted tones of the mine owners and the pit managers.

Annie May and Maggie never argued these issues because

the barrier between them was never a barrier. They were just friends, each reaching towards tomorrow and allowing yesterday to fade from their lives.

* * * * *

Something was different that day. There was, underneath Annie May's feet, a vibration that her well attuned deafness could not translate. There was a "sound" - unheard, but felt. Annie May could not translate it into words.

When she next met Maggie her only thought was that Maggie would explain the strange vibration that she had witnessed.

"Oh" said her friend, "a new brass band has been formed and they're using the Institute to practise. They're using the upstairs room".

Many Tuesdays followed that first one and on such a day Annie May was too late to present her book for renewal. She turned away from the closed door of the library and bumped into a middle aged, silvered haired gentleman who was carrying the case of a tenor horn. They apologised together.

Maggie met Annie May later and presented two tickets for a concert to be held in the Workman's Hall a fortnight to the day. Annie May did not object because they were friends.

She found a piece of lace and added it to the collar of the dress she had worn so long ago at Ifor's funeral. "I won't feel too much out of place" she said.

Maggie called for her that evening and for the first time in her life Annie May rode in a motor car. She did feel special and when the driver opened the passenger's door she might have been royalty.

The concert was certainly a successful occasion and although the singers were a little indistinct to Annie May's impaired hearing, the band's sound throbbed through her and her evening was complete. She thought the man with tenor horn - different.

She and Maggie discussed it at length at their next meeting and not for the first time in their relationship to date,

Maggie recognised Annie May's awareness, her intellect, her simple vision.

Tuesdays became important to Annie May. Of course, she could return and renew her books but she could also sit and feel the sound of the brass band's music one floor above. Often the duty librarian - even Maggie - advised her to go home but the rhythm and the throbbing through floor captured her and another avenue was opened to her. Ike had begun it, the choir in the Primitive Methodist had nurtured it but in that vibration Annie May "saw" anew.

One Tuesday, the resounding of "The Trumpet Voluntary" moved her and, to part from the outside door of the Institute seemed to Annie May almost a dereliction of duty. She did not want to remove herself from the lovely music that enchanted her.

Trombone players, euphoniumists, cornet players and even the conductor himself passed her by without disturbing her reverie.

"Sorry Missus" said a voice that bumped into her as she stood almost in shadow in the recessed doorway of the Institute. "I didn't see you there".

"My fault" said Annie May. "I should have been looking where you were going". Her flustered unwitting comment captured Harry - the tenor horn player. They had met before.

Harry was a shortish man, almost forty years old. Prematurely silvered hair had not detracted from his good looks but Harry preferred a bachelor's life. His interests were cricket, brass band and drinking beer - but not necessarily in that order. He worked as a miner but bachelorhood had not prompted him to seek promotion at his work place and he was content to receive his wages on Friday, play cricket on Saturday and be lucky to have enough to buy a couple of pints on a Monday.

"Where're you from then?" he asked and they discovered that to return home they would walk the same route and Harry would continue another mile or so when she turned into her adopted village.

"G'night, see you again sometime", were his parting words.

"That would be nice", she said.

See each other again they did, Tuesday after Tuesday after band practice and it was not until she arrived at the library some months later and read the large printed notice on the door cancelling the rehearsal, that she realised how much she looked forward to walking home with Harry.

Annie May looked forward eagerly to the following band practice - Tuesday - and when no vibrations reached her at their usual time, a host of butterflies invaded her stomach and it was Maggie, whom she met a day or two later who explained that the District Branch of the Miner's Federation had called special meetings to discuss the emergency that was brewing in the coal industry.

Harry, after rehearsal the following week, talked of hardly anything else as they renewed their regular walk homeward. He explained that pit closures in other coal fields in the north of England were creating unemployment in those areas and there was a fear that it would spread into the valleys of Wales.

The valley was built on coal. It provided houses, it provided work, it provided a living. True, life was very hard for those hardy people but coal cemented communities and created a closeness bred of their common need. Choirs and bands and debating societies and chapel congregations bore witness to the harmony of the people of the valleys - except for the outbursts that frequently occurred outside the pubs on Saturday night.

"With pit closing, families will have to live on less than 25 shillings a week", said Harry. "We musn't let the bloody mine owners win".

They had reached their parting point on their journey home and Annie May watched the solid man's shape move away as she readied herself to turn onto the hill road that would take her to the Manse, where she could sit and talk to the firelight.

"Oh! Annie May", called back Harry. "How would you like to go to the pictures on Saturday? Buster Keaton is on at the Olympia".

"I'd like that", she said.

The night at the pictures marked an unspoken change in their relationship. Harry walked her to the door of the Manse and boylike, kissed her on the cheek before he turned to walk the two miles home. Annie May retired to her room, lit the mantle of the gaslight and took down the cherished photograph of her lost one.

"You don't mind do you love?" she said.

Each week their meetings became more frequent and the minutes of company grew to half hours and longer. Annie May told Harry of her life to date; of her vision. Harry was preoccupied with the miners' woe but introduced Annie May to another world too.

She saw him score 58 runs against the local league champions and share in the honour that acclaimed it the best innings - not the highest score - that the valley had ever seen - even though the mysteries of that noble game would never be understood by a mere woman. The brass band she was much more akin to, because of Ike's musical interest; and when Harry's band combined in a concert in her home valley with another - to raise money for the Federation's funds - and Ike was the guest conductor, Annie May's heart was full. Martha Jane and her husband were there, as was Elsie. Leanna and Owen could not attend because of an imminent confinement but everyone thought that their "mother" was doing the right thing and putting the past behind her.

Annie May and Harry walked a lot - over the hills and down the valley - and everywhere there was evidence of the rape of that beautiful place. "God created this valley" said Annie May. "Look what you diggers in the earth have done to it".

"Not us" replied Harry. "Them bloody owners from England".

All around were the scars of industry - pyramids of coal slack that blocked out the green; stark pit head machinery, monuments to profits - but above all the blue marked, pinched faces of the men and the desperate faces of the women who bore the day to day agony and could do nothing to change their lot.

Early in the new year, Harry invited Annie May to a meeting in the Town Hall. The local MP was going to speak.

There was much ceremony from the local officials and Annie May doubted their motives but, when Mr. Evan Davies MP stood and warned the audience that they would get nothing from the Coal Commission's recommendations to abandon the less economic mines, she remembered Harry's words:

"With pits closing, families will have to live on less than 25 shillings a week" and her memory was rekindled and she remembered Dad's struggle and George's struggle and the Great War that would end all wars. "Why are we still at war?" she thought. "Only this time we are fighting our own people, not those 'over there'".

Next day she went to the library and proceeded to the 'Reading Room'. That is where the newspapers of the day were laid out on sloping stands and were available and free to all members of the Institute. Annie May had never been in that room to read before because "things were as they were and you just had to get on with it".

She found the local paper "The South Wales Argus" and searched until she saw Mr. Evan Davies MP reported from the meeting she had attended.

She read about abandoning less economic pits, saw him continuing to say that "It was not possible to have a national wages agreement if the industry was run by private enterprise in the way it was run today. The owners were anxious to get back to district areas in regard to wage agreements which would result in a reduction in wages. The only solution is for the Government to continue to subsidise or take over the industry".

If she did not understand all the words or the rhetoric, she understood the implications. Men would lose their jobs and women and children would go hungry.

Annie May exchanged no books at the library during the next months and did not meet with Maggie. After all Maggie was on the other side - she was the daughter of a manager. Instead, she met Harry and agreed with his point of view, reinforced by her frequent reading of the local newspaper.

March 11, 1926, The Argus reported the Royal Commission of the Coal Industry's recommendations:

1. An increase of an hour in a working day from 7 - 8 hours (at the coal face).
2. Reduction in wages.
3. Some economies in costs.
4. Large diminuation in railway rates by lowering railwaymen's wages.

A newspaper leader of the day perhaps best sums it up.

"The situation is very difficult. There are great obstacles to peace. Years of fear, suspicion, distrust - years in which there have been faults and wrongs on both sides - years in which the gap between the employers and the employed has widened. All have created an atmosphere which is not favourable to peace".

Martha Jane, with her husband, was in the thick of the battle and they were frequent visitors to Annie May and the ever present Harry, especially since the new Omnibus service had been introduced between the two towns. It cost only 1d (a penny) to travel four miles and it was only a penny ha'penny return. All four livened the life of the Manse, if not the life of the conservative Reverend Pearce with their political evenings, but news arrived that the omnibus had been involved in an accident - 'because the engine had malfunctioned' - and two were injured and one person was killed.

"Please God" prayed Annie May, "Let it not be Martha Jane and Cyril".

It was not, but the tragedy was only a pointer to the gathering storm clouds.

The Argus reported:

"The industrial sky is dark. The proceedings at the delegate conference of the Miner's Federation in London seem to be portents of a coming storm."

"The Miner's Federation referred the decision of the Coal Commissioner's recommendations to the districts but suggest:

(a) no increase in the working day.

(b) that the principle of national wage agreement with a national minimum wage be firmly adhered to.

(c) in as much as wages are already too low they cannot assent to any proposal reducing wages".

Annie May read words like deadlock, negotiations, executives, federations. They did not seem to her to refer to people, at least not to ordinary people. Perhaps people like the Member of Parliament and the Alderman and the Chairman of the Council and the Chief Librarian were important but what about Mrs. Pugh and her family of five? What about Evan Pritchard - who was not quite all there? What about Harry and her? Weren't they God's people too? Did they not have a place in His Kingdom on earth?

It did not seem as if they did and when Harry told her that a notice had been put up at the pit head which proclaimed that at the end of the month all existing terms and conditions would cease and that new terms would be posted on the 1st May 1926, Annie May knew for certain that in this world there were the chosen few who had and the ordinary people who had not.

Dark clouds indeed gathered over the valley. The forthcoming new terms and conditions were the sole topic of conversation.

Mrs. Pugh sobbed "For a full week Ossie brings home ú3 1s 0d after stoppages. Rent is £2 15s a month. We won't be able to carry on if wages is any less. What'll we do Annie May?"

No quarrels or fighting took place at the Inn those Saturday nights. Men talked politics, unanimous in their point of view.

"The Government is driving us into the ground. They don't give a bugger for us or ours. They're only interested in profits for the sodding owners" were typical heartfelt, table thumped versions of the feelings those dreadful days invoked. By the 1st May 1926, all the collieries in South Wales were stopped. The news of the breakdown in negotiations was taken calmly but everywhere there was an atmosphere of doom.

The men were on strike not only in the valley but throughout the land and the whole of industry ground to a halt. This was the General Strike of 1926.

Of course, as is the nature of such things, compromise was eventually reached. Both sides won and both sides lost but in the end, although wages were not cut, jobs were lost, pits were closed. Among those was Harry's pit and he did not work again for twelve years.

Harry was one of the lucky unemployed. He collected his pittance dole money but his four sisters doted on their young brother and they between them, did not let him go short.

There was Elizabeth (Lizzie) an angel in human form and Louisa, the workaholic and Martha Jane who was more deaf than Annie May - and there was Alice. Alice stood under five foot but her drive and the support from Caradoc (Crad) her husband transformed her into a giant and a book could be written about that particular lady.

Annie May lived the following year or so still attending chapel services regularly, still attending to her duties at the Manse, still visiting the library and renewing and expanding her reading scope - "Little Women" became a favourite - meeting Harry, of course, and sharing with him thoughts and hopes and promises that "all would come right in the end". She also served in the soup kitchen set up in the Chapel school room. Nervously she took Harry to The Nook, not expecting him to 'see' what she saw but in this she was mistaken. Harry's forty two years had been spent as a "bachelor gay" and cricket matches and boozing sessions afterwards might not have been an ideal preparation for an introduction to the poetry of The Nook, however, crudely Annie May presented it - but he was a sensitive man and life's true values were not lost on him. His dark brown eyes flecked with gold that reflected the silver of his hair, saw more than his tongue pronounced.

When, on a Summer's day in 1928, they wandered into the hills above Annie May's two valleys, she pressed on and reached the place that she had discovered fourteen years, a lifetime, earlier.

"Lovely spot isn't it Harry?" she pleaded.

"Yes love" he said. "Look at those streams there. Three into one".

She had had no doubts before and the four years they had known each other had been personally joyous, but now she was sure. Of course, social conditions and political controversy had made life hard but between her and Harry a bond had been formed and on that day by the side of Trinity the two became one.

They did not "have to get married" but they had to get married and plans had to be made.

She consulted Reverend Pearce, who approved but he did not think her quarters in the house would be sufficient for a married couple and promised he would make enquiries. Until they could find a home their plans would have to be set aside. Buying a property was beyond their scope. Perhaps rooms with someone who was struggling to pay off a loan? Renting, of course, was the best bet. But where?

No solution presented itself, though Annie May and Harry too and the Reverend Pearce searched every avenue.

"Hallo stranger", said Maggie one day as she and Annie May bumped into each other in the town market. "Maggie" said Annie May and they fell upon each other, the political differences forgotten as if they had never been.

"Let's have a cup of tea in the Faggots and Peas stall" invited Maggie. "My treat".

The 'cup of tea' became three cups and the friends were joyous to be together.

"How is Harry?"

"What have you been doing?"

"Read any good books lately?" They both laughed at that.

"Haven't been to The Nook".

"I have. Lovely place".

"Thinking of getting married".

The last came from Maggie. Mr. Meredith had joined the library staff - "Surely Annie May must have noticed him, although he was in accounts" - and he had invited Maggie to a performance of Iolanthe by the local G & S Society. "Well" she explained "One thing led to another and John had proposed to her and she had accepted. "Will you be my Maid of Honour?" she requested.

"I'll be delighted" said Annie May in a voice and a curtsey, way beyond her class.

The wedding was conducted - a bit stiffly - by the vicar of St. George's Church, or at least that is what Annie May thought but the day was a wonderful success and she delighted in the happiness of the bride and groom. In those times of austerity, the reception was a banquet and Annie May was glad for her friend.

Harry's questions to John proved to be most important of the day - or at least John's replies.

"Where are you gonna live?"

"We've bought a house near the park".

"Lovely. Where are you at the moment?"

"Oh, I rent a place up the spur. It's alright but Maggie and I want a place of our own".

"Anybody taking it on?" enquired Harry.

"I don't think so", said John. "Ask Maggie's dad, he owns it".

Ask Maggie's dad they did and it was agreed that when Annie May and Harry married they could have No. 5 for five shillings a week.

"I wish it was No. 1" said Harry. "Perhaps we could have that for a bob".

CHAPTER SEVEN

Bryn Bicca was a suburb of the village, reached along a lane, wide enough for two vehicles to pass and about 200 yards long and perched at the top of a steepish hill. In all there were nine houses. Five were strung together on a line still rising beyond the lane, with a sixth stuck to the end at right angles in the shape of an inverted capital L. Three others formed a small terrace, set a little apart from the main block as befitted dwellings that were posh because they had small stained glass patterns adorning their front doors. No. 5 was at the corner of the L. The hamlet was separated from the village by the fifteen acres of Ike Caswell's farm that catered for six dairy cattle, two dozen scraggy sheep and a few horses - although the latter were let loose to roam the hillsides and scavenge as meagre an existence as did the people from the industry denuded land.

Harry and Annie May's first visit to No. 5 was an adventure that they anticipated with excitement and as they climbed the hilly lane the sun shone, dispersed the fine rain and displayed a full rainbow that seemed like a covenant to the middle aged couple who soon were to begin a new life. They paused at the lampost. Gas filled, arms spread in welcome to all who ventured near but to that well met duo an omen. A sign that all that had passed had passed and their future was agreed and accepted by the hamlet's silent sentinel.

They passed No. 1 and Maisie Griffiths wished them well, Jack and Gwenny Price waved from the window of No. 2 and met them on the way back. Ossie Pugh, his wife, Gert, holding a curly headed baby John, Welsh style in a woollen shawl, invited them in to No. 3 for a welcoming cup of tea and when they knocked at No. 4 to get the key, that had been entrusted to Reg Hancock, they had become acquainted with every family of the L except Ma and Pop Taylor, who lived in the sixth house which could be reached only by going around the whole block.

No. 5 was a two-up and two-down dwelling introduced by a scullery, covered in tin sheetings, with a lead pipe served cold water tap, immediately in front of you as you crossed the threshold. Turning right, the happy couple viewed the living room - settled one step higher than the scullery - and saw that the black-leaded grate was two yards to the left and, further along the wall, another door led to a toilet.

"That's posh" said Annie May. "It's got a chain". The room was no more than ten feet by eight and diagonally across from the entrance was the staircase whose landing presented two bedrooms - one small and one smaller. Back in the living room - almost opposite the grate was the front room. How spacious and elegant it seemed, about ten feet by ten feet with a 'cwtch' in the corner and a nineteenth Century decorated ceramic fireplace taking the dominant spot.

The couple viewed the property with anticipation and expectancy. Their only question was, "How can we furnish such a mansion?" The question related not only to the requisite furniture but more importantly to the rental cost.

No answer immediately presented itself but over the following months a second hand sofa, a repossessed bed, several gifts from the family of money and goods, and pride of place, a leather covered armchair from the Reverend Pearce - never once regarded as a cast off - furnished all but the spare bedroom. From their combined finances - Annie May's meagre wages and Harry's eight bob a week dole money - they bought enough oil cloth to clothe the living room and the front room floors and set aside enough to invite twelve people to the register office wedding and pay 7/6d for the licence.

Maggie, of course, was Maid of Honour and John made them rich. He gave them a white £5 note. Harry said "I'll not take that". Annie May cried with gratitude, thanked her friends and set it aside for a "rainy day".

Saucepans, flat irons, sheets and pillow cases, blankets and an oil lamp came from the hard pressed families and the happy couple's day was complete.

That day, Harry was 43 and Annie May was 38 and they behaved like twenty year olds. Their first night in their new home was ....wonderful.

Married couples were entitled to twenty shillings a week from the Parish, cancelled if either party found employment. They were a little better off than some of their neighbours because of the concessionary rent charged by Mr. Weed, but of luxuries, there was none. Yet they found joy in each other. Harry adapted - with an effort - from his bachelor life, still played cricket for the town team and remained after matches only long enough to quench his thirst with two pints of the best. The brass band continued to flourish and Harry was a solid, loyal member if no virtuoso on the tenor horn. Annie May still changed her books on Tuesday, attended chapel on Thursday and twice on a Sunday. Harry did not adapt as much as all that.

"Chapel is for christenings, weddings and funerals" he said but he did accompany his wife to the midnight candle service on Christmas Eve and even put on his best white muffler (the only one he had) and wiped each toe of his boots on his trousers as he entered the double doors of the chapel. She had to nudge him to take his pipe from his mouth. "Sorry love" he whispered, "I forgot".

Together they made their little house a home. Spick and span it had to be, due to Annie May's habit of hard work and pride in service which had been part of her all her life and the black-leaded pebble at the doorstep glistened and often returned her thoughts to The Row. Harry dug the garden with little skill, not much enthusiasm but out of necessity and they struggled through their first year no better and no worse off than their neighbours and the increasing hordes of the unemployed but the first snows of their second winter heralded the true deprivation prevalent in that era. Harry, no longer a collier, was not entitled to free coal and the pittance they received from the grudging State did not run to renewing the meagre stock in the coalcot.

They were forced to wear outdoor clothes around the house and retire early as those warning flurries of snow blew into drifts outside and bitter winds drove the temperature to many degrees below zero.

With pick and shovel they joined dozens of others on the

slag tips and outcrop patches, desperately scraping through the frozen surface in the hope that two or three hours work would half fill a sack with low grade fuel that might sustain them for a day or two. A hero of the time was the police bobby - Sergeant Jenkins - who never seemed to be available when those pathetic folk carried home their illegal spoils.

"It'd be easier if we had a gambo" said Ossie Pugh. "Some old pram wheels and a couple of planks is all we'd need".

The suggestion followed an impromptu meeting by the men of Bryn Bicca as they gathered near the lampost when the thaw had set in. They had thought that, while the weather had turned milder, they could gang together and stock up their coal sheds and "Be ready for the next cold spell". 'Sailor' Griffiths would be in charge of construction; he had an extraordinary skill and could turn his hand to anything. Bill Denner - from No. 9 - had an old pram that his family had used for the same purpose, but if the planks could be found "We'll be able to cart five times as much" he agreed.

The problem. The planks!

The men went home to think about it but it was one of the wives who made the suggestion. Next to the school was a sub-office belonging to the colliery owner. The buildings were separated by a wooden fence. Already two or three pieces were missing. "They won't miss half a dozen more will they?" was the question that needed no answer.

After dark one evening, eight men could have been seen - if they had taken the main road - each carrying a plank and, courtesy of Mr. Shawcross (Pit owner) and the skill of 'Sailor' Griffiths, a splendid gambo made its way to the coal patches less than a week later. Within a month every coalcot was replete. There was no surplus timber. Planks also made good kindling.

The weather remained clement all the rest of the winter and their second wedding anniversary found them poor but relatively comfortable and adjusted and settled in their partnership.

Unemployment simply means that a man is not gainfully in work.

In those days it meant that a man was virtually sub-human because he could not provide the basic needs for his family. Their housing was slumlike, their subsistence was at starvation level and their future did not exist. No-one provided for the family except the man. It had been so, as long as anyone could remember in the valleys. Harry, new to the responsibilities of a wife and a home, was pained that he did not travel to a place of work each day. No matter that his employment since the age of thirteen had been in the "bowels of the earth". He had been a collier and a bachelor and had had the wherewithal to live a reasonable kind of life but now, his home and his wife were entitled to much more than they were getting. It ate into his dignity and a hatred began to grow inside him. Even the kind Mr. Weed - a workman too - took on the apparel of the moneyed class and Harry and others in Bryn Bicca joined in the "them" and "us" syndrome.

Annie May listened and agreed with most of the arguments but her answer did not lie in militancy. No, her way forward had been decided years before when, at that beautiful place, not too far away, she had "seen" the future road.

Of course, they needed money to get by and occasionally Annie May helped in the Manse and guiltily accepted a few pennies - even a shilling - in recompense. Harry - with no guilt at all - took whatever was offered and occasionally scored when the rag and bone man arrived and he had collected beforehand half a cartful of "any old iron".

At home, together, they remained united and if their love was different from that of Annie May and Ifor it was never compromised. They were middle aged and experienced people able - if not to forget - to put the past behind them. Their meagre home was a sanctuary where they met together. Their different interests - brass band, cricket, beer, books, choir, chapel, simply intermingled and neither person was critical of the other's pursuits.

They were happily married.

CHAPTER EIGHT

Insecurity and despair, in spite of their love nagged at the fabric of their lives and the lives of all their neighbours and fellow sufferers. Annie May and Harry had no children but around them children were born and had to be fed.

There was very little food to be had at home and Mr. and Mrs. Pugh and Jenny Price and all the Mams and Dads cried themselves to sleep many a night in their desperation to feed their children; that they went without themselves was never considered a sacrifice - simply a manifestation of "the way it was".

Harry, a kind and considerate man, was making adjustments that could not have been easy after 40 odd years of bachelorhood but one Friday afternoon - the day of the Parish allowance - he succumbed to the lure of gambling.

Men gathered in hollow places among the hills and "three card brag" and "pontoon" were the attractions of the day. If you won, five or ten shillings could be added to the family budget. Harry sought out such a school, that he had often joined in the days before his marriage. That day "I'll only go and look", he whispered in his head. His good friend Clarence sat in a lucky spot and Harry sat behind him. No-one outside the game was allowed to comment but Harry noticed that the cards were falling Clarence's way and when his friend withdrew - better off by almost nine shillings - Harry knew that the fates had been kind and that he would never have a chance like this again.

Jacks and picture cards fell to him like rice at a wedding and his pile reached more than four pounds - a fortune, four week Parish.

Two hours later, Harry made a journey up the lane and put on the table, scrubbed white by Annie May - one shilling and six pence. It had been the only time Annie May saw Harry cry and she cradled him in her arms and said, "You did your best love".

That same year, the weather was worse than unkind - not

in winter but late in the springtime. Winds began to blow. No. 5 was not affected save for one tin sheeting lifted off the scullery roof, but down the spur and half a mile onwards to the North, where huts had been erected in 1919 as a temporary accommodation for returning heroes, things were very different.

Four of the wooden structures were lifted bodily and deposited as firewood three hundred yards away. Twenty more were damaged beyond repair.

Almost one hundred people lost their homes - mams, dads and kids.

The Reverend Pearce in chapel that Sunday read "Thus abideth, faith, hope and charity. And the greatest of these is charity".

Annie May thought that charity was not to be accepted because "It makes you like one of the lowest", she had always said. That day she understood that the proper interpretation of "charity" is love.

The community did love and each gave what it could. There was no money but there was kindness and concern and sharing and community.

The year did not improve. There was an accident with the trams at Ty Tryst - the only colliery still operating - about three months after the windy storm. John and Vic Alexander, the father and son at No. 8 Bryn Bicca had lost their lives and suffered the indignity of being brought home, still in their black and in their working rags, to be laid on the kitchen floor.

The tiny community could find no words to express its grief. Annie May searched her poetry books and her memory and talked to Harry and even coined a couplet or two but when she met Mrs. and the two bereaved girls she could only say, "I'm so sorry!"

Two years after their instalment in No. 5, Gert Pugh gave birth to a daughter, Rosina.

Annie May remembered Ruth! The hurt and the despair returned and for weeks she even shut out Harry, who manlike, had no idea of the yearning she experienced. To lose a child, at whatever age, must be the most devastating of human experience. "To outlive your child" said Annie May "was beyond understanding".

There were more children born, of course, Gordon and Bernard and Edith and Graham and Margaret and Nancy but all to the other families of Bryn Bicca. Annie May was forty one years old and beyond safe child bearing.

She rejoiced in the joy of the Pugh's and the Griffith's and the Hancock's and the Denner's and the Cartwright's - they lived in posh No. 7.

Annie May's dreams had died with Ruth twenty years earlier.

CHAPTER NINE

A family reunion was arranged. Ike, Martha Jane, Leanna, Annie May together decided to commemorate the anniversary of the break up of their home in The Row. Twenty five years had passed since Dad and George and they had been together.

Supper was arranged in Owen's and Leanna's house and all the families were invited. Annie May and Harry walked almost eight miles to be there, since they were a valley away and Owen arranged transport home. What a repast they enjoyed. Ham and tongue and even turkey and the inevitable pickles and several bottles of sherry were available. Harry did not like sherry but drank it "just to be sociable". Annie May ate her meal but felt a little nauseous.

The return home, perhaps because of the jolting of the motor car, only served to make her condition worse and next day Harry insisted that his ghost like wife stayed in bed.

One day in bed was enough for Annie May. In spite of her 'not total recovery' she applied herself to her chores around the house, her reading and her chapel commitments. "A bit of sickness is neither here nor there" she said.

Sure enough, three weeks later all adverse symptoms had disappeared. The only indication that things were different was one Sunday morning she had to breathe in hard to get on her best skirt to go to chapel.

At forty one years of age Annie May was pregnant. She and Harry received the doctor's confirmation with joy but a baby at 42, in 1933 was not without risk and danger. The whole family was delighted at the news and made more regular visits to make sure that the sister, who had been their mother all those years ago, was taking care of herself and they helped her to prepare for the big event.

The sisters, Leanna and Martha Jane, did not forget Annie May's first child - that beautiful little girl - who had been snatched away so cruelly. But they never reminded her of that. Instead they set to and transformed the second bedroom into a nursery. Oilcloth appeared and they did allow Harry to help in laying it on the bedroom floor. They let him carry the second hand or was it third hand (?) rocking crib up the stairs but that was the lot. "Men can't be expected to know about these things", said Martha Jane.

Annie May bloomed and Harry rejoiced in her joy. They talked long about this son that was to come to them so late in life. But they were not blinded to the quality of their life or to what they would be able to offer their newborn son.

"Things gone by seem like yesterday, but things to come seem like never coming" said Harry one evening during a game of dominoes. Annie May seemed always to win when they played "first out" but Harry was best at "fives and threes" and his philosophical interruption that evening under the mellow yellow of the brass oil lamp caused him to play a six/three that gave Annie May victory with a double six.

"He'll be here in less than a month" said Harry's wife.

And so he was, a six pound eight ounce boy whose eyes of Annie May blue, dimples and curly blonde hair captivated every mother who saw him. Annie May agreed with them all and rejoiced in her new born. Bath time was a joy and feeding. Simply watching that tiny scrap filled her days and half her nights. Harry was dutiful and did as he was told in respect of his son. After all, as Martha Jane had reminded him "Men don't know about these things".

The first month sped by and if the extra three shillings a week allowed them by the Guardians, did not provide adequately even for such a little soul, Annie May and Harry simply tightened their belts a little more. To Annie May the first four even five weeks were spent as if on some wondrous cloud and when she spoke sharply to Harry a day or two later and introduced their first quarrel in the five years of their marriage, Harry was bewildered, angry and hurt and retreated to the pub where he proceeded to drink too much - both for sobriety's sake and for the state of their purse.

He returned home late, still angry and not caring that Annie May would be worried. When he stamped through the door, Annie May had baby Charles settled to her breast. The shadows cast by the old oil lamp enhanced a picture of tranquillity that an artist would have been pressed to capture and Harry's head cleared and his heart softened as he knelt at his family's feet and wept his regret and his love. Annie May encircled them both with comforting arms. But during the next few days she seemed preoccupied. Although she "saw to" things around the house, to Harry's simple needs and to her baby son, her mind seemed to be elsewhere and when in the early hours of Sunday morning she was not beside him, Harry found her standing by Charles' crib wet with tears, reflected by the wax night light, as she looked at her beloved son.

"What's the matter May?" asked the mere man.

"It's his sixth Sunday" she replied "and I've been remembering little Ruth".

History did not repeat itself and the imaginings and the remembering during the past week were set aside and life in No. 5 returned to its former state - happiness in each other and in their son, in spite of their poverty and hardship.

Winter was kind that year and in the healthy December air the trio could be seen together on the lower hills, reddening their faces in the cold breeze and letting the unpolluted air fill their baby's lungs to make him strong and help him to grow.

At home they never let the boy go short of milk or sop and if they shared one faggot spread on bread, bought at Jack Short's corner shop just down the hill, to satisfy their evening hunger they were well rewarded. The six and a half pounds birth weight increased weekly and those blue eyes missed no movement as Mammy and Daddy talked to and played with and nursed and held the little bundle. Nurse Collins had visited and Annie May, a child of the nineteenth Century had asked "Can the baby catch the deafness from me?"

"You were not born deaf", explained the gentle nurse. "So it can't be hereditary..... he can't catch it". Annie May was reassured since she trusted the splendid practitioner, but often she would creep behind her son as he lay, and later sat, and click her fingers to be delighted as he turned to meet the sound and reward her with a chuckle.

It was expected that the child should be christened into the Methodist faith and Annie May set a date, 1st March. St. David's Day.

The family had always rallied round but this day belonged to the three from the corner house of the capital L and they would accept no help. How they would manage, what with a christening robe and flowers for the chapel and new clothes and the services and a tea, neither knew but manage they would.

Harry sat or rather played with the baby when she scrubbed the Manse and he walked, carrying his son, while she relieved a sick washerwoman in the town workhouse. Harry collected scrap and did two illegal stints on the vegetable cart that, horse drawn, plied its meagre trade from street to street. They put a little less on their table, they fuelled their fire sparingly and retired earlier to save on paraffin for the lamp.

In a month they had saved one pound three shillings and four pence and the crocheted robe alone was priced at eighteen shillings and six pence.

"What else can we do Harry?" asked Annie May. "Mary Jones is back in the laundry tomorrow. So I'm finished up there".

"I don't know May fach", he answered "but I'll think of something".

He did! Two days later he gave Annie May four one pound notes.

"Where'd you get.....?" she began.

"Ike the Pawn bought the tenor horn", Harry interrupted. "It's not as important as our little son, is it fach?" he asked. There could be no answer.

Annie May bought the christening gown and some bootees and a new hat with flowers on its rim for herself. Harry bought two collars and a pair of brown boots and Annie May exhausted the heat of six flat irons to make her Sunday best and Harry's ill matched suit ready for the occasion. They accepted nothing from anyone that day - except that Harry had to borrow a back stud from Reg next door when he found that he had mislaid his own, that he had not worn since his wedding day.

The christening was dignified and well attended, the Minister read the 23rd Psalm. All the sisters and in-laws were there - Leanna with young Glyn toddling at her side and Maggie and John, the baby's godparents. Later the little house was filled with people - family, neighbours and friends and they tucked into the feast that was provided. The baby was as good as gold and Annie May said to Harry, as they retired that night "My cup runneth over".

Tomorrow came and nothing was changed.

The valleys were barren places where old men sat on benches and steps of buildings and simply waited to die. Middle aged men hoped for a future that might restore their former life style - meagre though it had been. Young men had no hope at all. Families perished but some survived and the salt that spiced survival was love and community and "not letting the buggers beat us down".

Annie May and Harry and Charles were engulfed by love. The little family saw what passed around them but they were cocooned in an envelope called No. 5. When the door was closed of an evening, poverty and want never intruded, because the adult players had one aim in mind. To prepare for their son's future. Annie May was the more articulate in this respect as they lay side by side but Harry had not lived almost half a century without learning a little of life.

"Things will get better" he said "and the boy will be alright".

Annie May agreed but she knew the channel by which that dream could be realised.

CHAPTER TEN

In the January, after their son's third birthday, fulfilment of the dream began. Annie May took Charles to school.

The elementary school stood next to the pit owner's office but also hid The Nook, that had for so long been Annie May's refuge. To her mind there was a poetry in their juxta position. Beauty of The Nook married to the knowledge that the school could provide equated to an educated child - her son.

She saw to it that he was never absent. The headteacher certainly approved of that - not least because his salary depended on the attendances of his pupils. Annie May walked and carried her son every day at 8.30 a.m. towards the school and at home time, home again for not less than five years. During that period Charles, that little boy, missed two sessions of schooling.

Annie May still visited the library - fitting her attendance in with her son's presence at school and Harry joined her. He spent most of the time in the Reading Room and read of happenings in foreign lands, especially in Russia and Germany where opposing forces seemed to be creating - "I don't know what".

"Do you think there'll be a war?" she asked after such a session at the library. Her question took her back for once in recent years, to those things that had affected her life twenty years before.

But other things demanded recognition on the front pages of the press.

Words like, Coronation, Divorce, Abdication. They confused the common people who did not relate to the situation. But loyalty and country and sacrifice were what their fathers had given their lives for and were dear to the hearts of those abused common folk.

"Let the government sort it out" was as close as most valley people got to articulating their analysis for they believed in King and Country and in some indefinable system that was out there - somewhere. Village life remained the same. Football was played and cricket in their season. Chapel differed not at all and hell and damnation still dictated how men and women should think if not quite how they actually behaved but the forces of government still deprived those noble people of dignity and self determination and even a basic standard of living.

Harry and his wife and their son endured it all. But they survived because their life was based on the greatest of God's gifts. Given by a God - that Harry at the same time denied but sometimes accepted and even quoted.

"And the greatest of these is charity".

There was division between man and wife because Harry was practical and pragmatic and Annie May's foresight dwelt in the realms of hope and dreams bred in her vision of longings. Their son was too young to express an opinion but the differing points of view never intruded in the harmony of their love.

Charles' entry into school eased their financial burden, for each child received an enamel cup full of milk and a slice of bread at eleven a.m., if they attended school and that same mug was replenished with vegetable soup at midday. That made the difference between hunger and starvation.

The child blossomed. All those around him were captivated by his cherubic looks and some recognised a quality that they could not articulate. It did not originate in the child but rather in the special nature of the parents. Annie May had been a mother for thirty years before she gave birth to her first born son and Harry had experienced everything that a bachelor could experience in those innocent days, save parenthood. The little boy was their hope and their escape.

Holidays were non-existent, but once a year, the Chapel arranged a visit to the seaside. A saved up penny a week per person, guaranteed a trip on the charabanc to Barry Island - dream land - where all was bright and light and gay and magical. The little family joined in and all was as they had expected it to be. Candy floss, sand in their sandwiches, no room between the seats for legs, a half pint of beer and above all escape from their dreary existence.

Where fairground rides transported you to distant lands, simply excited your inner fancies and made you sick, or offered "Something for nothing" when you "Have a go Mister or Miss".

Annie May and Harry indulged themselves and spent sixpence on a studio photograph - of their son. He sat on a grey artificial rock, with artificial clouds painted behind his head, dressed in matching woollen jersey and shorts with the customary sandals. They thought, when they received the print, that their boy looked like a cherub.

Some years later, the photograph was enlarged and framed and took central position in their modest home.

The boy grew as the country grew and he knew nothing of the struggle around him, but his fourth birthday heralded a turn of the tide for Annie May and Harry and most of the downcast people of that dreadful time. There was talk about building a factory in the next valley. Annie May's home. Limestone and iron ore readily available in those rich hills could be combined with the abundant water to produce - STEEL.

The steelworks would need men to build it and labour to run the place.

Harry was among the first to apply to dig into the mountainside, to remove soil, to haul rocks, to fetch and to carry but - he was refused. The Irish immigrants were more experienced in the skills that the McAlpine construction company needed. So for more than a year nothing changed for the little family, but across the world, events were having an effect. Who could have seen them then? Certainly not the folk living in poverty in that tiny hamlet.

"Germany is a long way away".

"Chamberlain seems to have it all under control!"

"There still isn't enough food around to satisfy the family".

"Only the moneyed people have any say in anything".

"One day we'll have a government who gives a shit for us".

They were hungry and they were dispirited and their only hope, for those who attended, was in the religion of the day where salvation would be theirs if only they believed. But there was a tiny core of political animals who believed that equality could only be achieved through destruction of the ruling classes. "Had it not been proved in Russia" they asked.

Annie May and Harry - after Charles was safely in bed - asked the same questions. They never agreed on the how but they were totally of one mind and agreed that the last ten years especially, and the forty years before, had been an appalling experience for ordinary folk and somehow, tomorrow should be better for their son.

The terrible irony is, that in 1939, when three quarters of the world became engaged in an obscene war, when atrocities beyond the scope of human belief were being perpetrated, when at its end it cost 20,000,000 lives, when cities were razed to the ground and loved ones everywhere were sacrificed, the war was a blessing to Annie May and Harry and little six year old Charles.

Mert Jones had played cricket with Harry, but in the Spring of 1939 he was in too much of a hurry to stop and recall past glories in the most glorious of games. "Haven't you heard, there's jobs in the new steel works Harry? Construction is nearly finished and then they're sending the Irish back where they came from".

Harry sent a message with young John Pugh, so that Annie May would not worry, and joined Mert and William and Tom, Dick and Harry and five thousand more on the five mile trek over the mountain and down to the General Offices of Richard Thomas and Baldwin's brand new steel factory.

A month to the day the furnaces roared and at night time filled the sky with a redness that matched a sunset but heralded a dawn for those long suffering souls. Undermanned and closed pits saw the pit head wheels turn again to feed the mouths of the "open hearths" where iron mixed with limestone to boil and mingle and produce the steel that the world would soon need. And the work filled the brown envelopes on Fridays. Harry - now an engine cleaner in the "loco" shed - placed his first pay packet for twelve years onto the scrubbed table and he and Annie May stared at it, as if afraid that it was not real or that it might disappear and they each said thank you to his own God. Two younger eyes watched the scene and thought, "It must be funny to be a grown up".

In the first four weeks Harry's pay topped fifteen pounds - a fortune compared with the £1.7s.6d per week they had been receiving recently but the only things that changed in No. 5 were more food on the table and new clothes for the boy. Annie May started "putting something by" in the National Savings Cerstificates" (she never did get the pronunciation right) and she and Harry and Charles made a special visit to Mr. Weed, Maggie's father, taking with them the rent book. They had never missed a payment in eleven years that they had lived in their home and they were forever grateful for the reduced rent that the kind man had charged them.

"We've brought you a brier pipe, to say thanks" said Harry. "and from now on we are going to pay the proper rent of ten and six a week" finished Annie May.

Life for the family was moved into a different sphere. They were 'rich' people. Around them other families benefited too but when husbands and sons were deemed to be of military age, or when "glory" directed that men should enter the lists of chivalry, Annie May, in her inner self, was glad that Harry was too old and Charles too young to tread those desolate places from which few returned.

A pattern was established when Harry was put on 'nights' by the powers that were in R.T. & B's.

At eight o'clock, with little Charles in bed, the happy couple shared an extra meal - usually toast with cheese on top, "Welsh Rarebit" and sometimes a poached egg as well. Harry turned as he reached the plateau by the lampost and waved and always, Annie May blew him a kiss.

In the morning, Harry returned and a welcome cup of tea and, bacon or eggs according to rationing restrictions, sustained the well deserved sleep that the night shift demanded.

The mother tended her son. She woke him at a quarter past eight. She washed him and dressed him. She provided his morning meal. She accompanied him to the gates of learning that was the local Elementary School and, with doubt and fear and expectancy and hope and other undefined emotions, Annie May entrusted her beloved son into the arms and the minds of the teachers who practised their arts in that place of learning.

The five hours that he was out of her sight were a sort of punishment to her but it did not prevent her from returning day after day so that her dream could be realised.

Day after day the pattern continued. Harry worked from 10.00 p.m. until 6.00 a.m. He walked four miles each way.

Annie May prepared for her loved ones. Harry's box was cut. Charles' clothes and his food and his accompaniment to school were never neglected. Their home was improved, although their savings were not allowed to be diminished. Financially they were, by thrift, as well off as any other family in the village.

Emotionally they lived in the "little paradise". They simply were in love with each other. Father, mother and beloved son - the third Trinity.

Annie May realised where they were, because she had "seen" these things so many years ago. Harry had little time to dwell on philosophy. All he wanted to do was to make up for a gross of months when no one would employ him, when he starved and when he saw great men die because lesser men had more money. Charles was just a little boy.

Beyond their ordinary understanding was a world-wide vista. The sloping shelves of the library and the front pages of the "Daily Herald" that they now could afford, presented a comprehensive picture of world affairs. Harry and Annie May read each page with interest but nothing that was reported changed their point of view.

"We live here", they said. "We must look after the place. Charles must have a better life than us".

All these happenings seemed only to be channels for Annie May's dream. Somewhere inside her psyche each step had been planned. The period that had passed and the incidents that had occurred had all contributed to the present.

Her mother had died young. She had taken on the responsibility.

Dad had wasted away but his end had strengthened her resolve. The firelight had shown her the way forward. George had provided and Ike and Martha Jane and Leanna had rewarded her ambition for them.

Necessity had prompted her choices and tragedy had directed her into a new valley, another place, a distant land just five miles away from her birth place. There she had found channels to relieve her search. Maggie and Harry and brass bands and hunger and love and above all, her little son. She could never have put those forty years into words but "tomorrow is another day" she said and she was never more sure of anything than when she tucked her little boy safely in his bed and stretched up tall and whispered for fear of wakening him. "You'll have an education, my boy" and she stooped and kissed her baby.

Two years into their affluence, when the whole of Europe was under the jack booted heel of a tyrant, when standing on their doorstep of a late evening they could see, if not hear, the distant sights of bombardment twenty miles to the South of Newport, Annie May and Harry thanked God that the war seemed not to touch their little home directly.

The war affected them both economically to their advantage, but philosophically, changed their perspective not at all.

"Look love" said Harry. "We've had years of going without and we've got to look after ourselves".

"No" said Annie May with a strength of conviction that prompted Harry's point of view.

"We've got to make it better for the boy" she said.

CHAPTER ELEVEN

In the way of things, two situations arose. Annie May had a whitlow on her finger that was extremely painful. Harry arrived home from work one morning to find his wife barely coping with the routine of the day.

"Sorry love" she said, "I haven't slept all night. This thing on my finger is awful bad. I can't bear to touch it".

Harry cooked the breakfast and took Charles to school. He returned and made sympathetic noises and even took the brush and swept the living room floor. Without sleep he made his usual journey to his place of work and prayed that tomorrow would see an end to the lump on Annie May's finger. But his prayer was unanswered - if anything the swelling was worse and Annie May was certainly not herself. She lay on the sofa nursing the offending limb, although she had seen the boy off to school and Harry - exhausted - decided that he would take a night off to care for his little family.

* * * * *

A clock-watcher could set the time by Harry's routine.

At eight o'clock he waved to Annie May, by the lampost. Four miles later he arrived at Tamplin's Vaults and had one pint of bitter. Occasionally he increased his intake by another half but always arrived at the clocking in point in the loco shed at ten minutes to ten and, after a quick brew of tea with the outgoing shift, earned the wages like a good 'un.

* * * * *

That night exhaustion defeated his resolve and Harry slept with his wife for the first night since 1939.

At eight twenty at the gate of Isle's Farm, at the actual point and at the actual time that Harry usually passed, a German pilot decided to drop a bomb - probably too heavy a load to return to the Fatherland.

Harry was not there and was not buried in the twenty foot crater that was the source of interest for dozens of souvenir hunters and other interested folk.

Annie May's whitlow was a blessing. She believed it. Harry said it was a coincidence.

War affected everyone but, the little family escaped the peril and hardship of thousands of their compatriots because they had no representative in their family risking his life in a foreign land and work, so long unobtainable, provided a good life for the dwellers in No. 5.

Summer followed Spring and the essence of Autumn enhanced the insight of all who were observant, but Winter that year treated the whole community to a harsh lesson. None more than Annie May and little Charles.

Harry had left to find his way to the Steelworks at eight o'clock as usual and had arrived on time at "Clocking In" several minutes before penalties would be exacted from his pay packet and he spent the night simply doing his job.

Annie May had seen to the evening needs of herself and her son who went to bed at nine, sewed a button on Harry's shirt, read a chapter of her recent acquisition from the library, read the message in the grate, that still was her source of inspiration and had lain down to a well deserved sleep to prepare for the welcome of her husband at about seven in the morning.

At eight o'clock, Annie May had Charles almost - apart from giving him his breakfast - ready for school. Harry had not arrived home. Outside the terrace, snow drifted to two or three feet but at that elevation above sea level that was not unusual. She took her son to school, since schooling was more important than a little wind and a drift or two but when ten o'clock struck by the pendulum clock that affluence had provided for them, anxiety crept into Annie May's heart. Harry should be home by now.

Harry had left his place of work at 6.10 a.m., loitered a little to discuss things with his friends and work mates but his journey home had been diverted by wind and gale and snow and an hour later, he found himself lost 1500 feet above sea level, ill equipped to deal with conditions that would have tested seasoned mountaineers. The white out destroyed his sense of direction and although he strayed not more than a few degrees from his selected path he ended up on a mountain at Monmoel, five miles from his destination.

A farmer, down the valley, searching for lost sheep, saw a white black shape huddled in a mountain hollow that was almost filled with snow. Harry owed his life to Idwal Morgan and Annie May remembered the message of hope that the dwindling fire in the grate had presented to her a night ago.

"Where's daddy?" asked the little boy Charles on the journey to school.

Harry was put to bed at about three o'clock in the afternoon, he stirred in time to go on the night shift but remained in the bed and failed to report at "Clocking In" for only the second time in his second working career.

CHAPTER TWELVE

The war continued its carnage and its evil ways and the end seemed no where near but it provided - for three days - a brother for the little boy at No. 5. Annie May took Charles "down the school" on a Friday evening and waited for an hour or more with all the village mothers and a few dads too. At last a bus pulled up outside the school gates and from it alighted a company of young children and two adults. The children were strangely alike. All wore outdoor clothes, carried a paper parcel or small cardboard case in one hand, a brown gas mask suspended around their necks and, in their lapels dangled a luggage label proclaiming the child's name. The sameness of their appearance was matched by the pain and tiredness and the apprehension and the lostness that marked each of those unhappy souls, who had waved and sobbed "Goodbye" to their parents in far away London early that morning. The "vacees" had arrived.

Bomb torn London had sent its children to a safe place and the valley was their haven. What they thought of their "new parents" cannot be described. Comparisons were only possible inside the heads of those war torn children.

Whatever had been their pre-war lot they were ill prepared for this different place. Tenement or terrace or semi or detached belonged to a different world. They heard new accents, even a new language, and none of these eased the pain of parting from whence they came.

First, they were made to assemble in the largest classroom of the school. Comforted by the two teachers who had alighted with them from the bus. They were called for a drink and a currant bun in alphabetical order and enjoyed the small luxury. "Better than the bloody bombs, 'en it?" said a ringer for Dicken's Artful Dodger, while others clung to their friends and spilled tears from an already empty well.

Eli Meyrick, the headmaster, related to those other Meyricks that Annie May had known a lifetime ago, welcomed the visitors and hoped that they would be happy and soon settle in the valley that was only too eager and pleased to receive them.

A name was called but it nominated a girl. Mrs. Griffiths had wanted a boy "I'll taker her" said Mrs. Snelgrove. Mrs. Hale took one of each. Shuffled they were from those and them until almost all that flotsam was taken into a sheltering harbour.

Well! Almost all, but not the boy with the hare lip or the girl with the cabbage face and Derek Windibank - what an English name - was sent back on the next transport. "Who wanted to look after a loony?"

But Annie May's and Charles' nomination was ideal. He was the same age as Charles and his family was working class. Dad worked in the docks. His elder brother was housed with Gwenny Price, just three houses away. What could be a better arrangement?

"Plumduff", the name that was later bestowed on the slightly tubby lad, was incurably homesick.

Annie May's motherliness, Harry's afternoon attempts at walks and talks in the surrounding district, Charles' experience in school or childish secret places never could overcome that lost child's roots and three days later he joined his brother at Gwenny's place and before Christmas he returned with 95% of those victims of power seekers, to his home that had sought his safety, had sacrificed his contact. With heartache and much anguish and joy the Reunion said "'ope you've 'ad a good 'oliday".

Annie May felt a failure but knew that you could not always win and she had to make that clear to her little son.

He never felt lonely, because his parents put him first. Alright, Dad was mostly in bed. Sometimes though Harry took the boy to a cricket match and every day in Summer found time to tell him of past glories and the majesty of this most majestic of games. "Jack Hobbs was the greatest that would ever be". "Yes" there was a great pause always. "Len Hutton scored 364 at The Oval, that's the highest ever in test cricket. But Jack Hobbs is the best that will ever be" he insisted.

Charles' greatest moment was when he hit his Dad for four consecutive fours when he bowled at him against the lampost with a bat that Dad had fashioned from an old plank.

Harry never rehearsed his son in the intricacies of a musical score but the tip tap of his fingers or the rhythms when a song was sung or a wireless played - they did not acquire one because of Annie May's deafness - made Charles aware of that divine muse. And on occasions Annie May took her son to Ike's house, which was dominated by melodic sound. She took him to chapel and the choir master found him a song to sing in the Sunday School Anniversary.

The boy thought that he would become another Ike. He was wrong! But all these things instilled an awareness in the child and Annie May directed all these things. She did not direct world events, of course, but she found in them persuasions and directions and insights.

She did not read a musical score but she ensured that her son would be exposed to their influence. Her reading was quite extensive although often times over her head but if she could arrange its availability for her son, then she was on the way to fulfilling her vision of long ago.

With this in mind, she paid a rare visit to Maggie's house.

They greeted each other with arms and kisses and genuine friendship. Annie May felt not the least bit out of place when Maggie produced tea and sandwiches on bone china. After all, Annie May was used to such luxury. She had carried it into the tea rooms of at least three tea rooms a hundred times in her "skivvy" days.

Neither was Maggie perturbed. Their different backgrounds had never intruded and never could they or would they.

"Maggie" said Annie May, when tea was almost over "Tell me what to do for the boy".

The answer did not immediately emerge. Maggie sat back and drank another cup of tea. Of course, she offered the same to her welcome guest. Then Maggie made a speech.

"Ladies and Gentlemen" she almost said but there were only two ladies present. "Ladies and Gentlemen, here we have a seven year old boy. Born into poverty, but born into a family - which will win? Poverty or Family?

"In between we are surrounded and directed by forces that drive the world to total chaos. Each side proclaims that it is right. They actually pray to the same God.

"What shall we tell this little boy to do?"

"We are involved in different values. If you own a million pounds and a grand estate then you are rich. If you own nothing and cannot find a crust for your next meal. You are poor. That is the way the world judges your success".

"I had that" said Maggie "until that rotten bastard in Cardiff changed my point of view". She went on. "Annie May, owning things can never ever be important. Look for something beyond today for your little boy and tomorrow he will reap the reward".

Maggie answered the question and left Annie May to return to No. 5 as bemused as she had been when she sought her friend's help. "Harry" she pleaded "please help".

Harry worked seven nights a week in the loco shed. He won back the dignity that had been stolen from him by twelve years of forced idleness. He understood Annie May's dream but did not see as she saw, and the contribution he made to his son's upbringing was to provide for their physical needs and talk man's talk to the little boy. When the little group walked on the hillside, Annie May took a book for her son to share or stopped and picked a wild flower and, although rarely could she name the species, the shape and the delicacy and the miracle of its life was explained to young Charles ineloquently, but it registered in his young fertile mind.

While Annie May prepared the picnic, Harry would skim stones across Blue Lakes calm waters and challenge the boy to beat his record of thirteen "ducks and drakes". He talked about work and security and even mentioned education. But sport and manly pursuits were his goals for his son. But he added kindness and caring, because he was kind and he cared. He taught the lad to finger a scale on his parted tenor horn by use of the knuckles of his three middle fingers C.D.E.F.G.A.B.C. and the boy never forgot.

Annie May cherished those years when her husband was fulfilled, when the larder was full, when her son was being prepared. The war was a distant happening for her. She grieved and remembered, when news arrived of yet another casualty, but rejoiced that none of hers was involved. Ifor had been enough.

1942 dawned! The end was three years away. Stalingrad, Pearl Harbour, D-Day, unconditional surrender. VJ Day.

Streets were decked with bunting. Parties lasted all day and all night but Annie May celebrated the end of the war without Harry.

1942 dawned! She rose at the usual time. She prepared the morning meal for her son and husband, sent Charles to school and assumed that Harry had worked on a bit, to earn some extra, but at half past nine that May morning Harry Cartwright, The Shop, who had a telephone, knocked at the door of No. 5 Bryn Bicca.

"Missus Hawkins" he started, "Harry's been taken bad at work. He's in the General. They didn't tell me what was wrong".

She caught the Red and White bus to the hospital where Harry lay with an abscessed bladder.

"It'll be alright love" she said echoing the words of long ago.

But again she was wrong.

Harry died of poisoned kidneys due to septicaemia.

CHAPTER THIRTEEN

Some days after Harry's funeral, Annie May arose very early. Charles would stay in bed because of the Christmas holidays. The fire was stubborn and would not turn from smoke into flame. She took the double pages of the Daily Herald and used them as a blazer. Someway through its quest, the newsprint spoke to Annie May. It caught in the early flames of the morning fire and left were the remains of the headline which read "Alive". That it referred to an enemy plane shot down and that the pilot had been captured alive registered not at all in Annie May's mind. When she saw the flame digested newsprint shedding its carbon flakes, backed by a steady firelight glow which silhouetted a replica of her dead husband, she knew that he was alive........ somewhere. He and the firelight had spoken to her again as it had done a hundred times before.

She sold Harry's few possessions. His only good suit. His cricket bat of 15,000 runs. His half pint pewter tankard she had bought him for his 50th birthday - making it a half to help him beat the "demon drink". She sold his hardly worn brown boots and remembered the day he had first worn them. "What a day that had been", she remembered. But the memory of Charles' christening and Harry's shining boots brought on a sudden cold and twice she blew her nose and she cursed..... "Damn and blast", she cried.

One week later Harry appeared to her. Not as a spirit nor as an image nor as a man. Simply as a memory. She needed to light the old brass oil lamp and took a paper spill from the brass holder on the mantelpiece. All three of the family had turned them together, from strips of the daily newspaper. They saved the matches especially when Harry needed to light his old "ronk" pipe. Her eye fell on the Scotty Dog pipe rack and the three briers that rested therein. She took the curved yellow stemmed favourite and fondled it, caressed it, made love to it and remembered - Harry.

The next day she took her son aside and gave him a present. "Don't you forget your daddy".

He never has!

* * * * *

Annie May was reduced once more to life alone - she did, of course, have her son. She had to look after him and her dream, as a widow, on a widow's pension. Life became hard again. Her savings were soon gone and she returned to the life she knew best. The life of hard work. Scrubbing and washing and cleaning - for other people - so that she could supplement the pittance that the State awarded.

Visits to the library were less frequent, but, when she went, she took Charles with her and developed in him a love of books and a realisation that there was a life outside the valleys and a channel by which such a life could be achieved. Annie May's dream was well on the way.

Day to day children's squabbles were dealt with - often unfairly. The problem of living, i.e. enough to eat and warmth and clothes were almost insurmountable for a person in Annie May's position at that time. How could a widow live - with a child - on £1 a week, when the rent alone was ten shillings and six pence? How could a widow with Annie May's vision provide for her son's future?

But Annie May saw, as she had seen so long ago, the avenue of escape from that hemmed in world that her experience had dictated to be her destiny.

The answer was in a word or two. Work and Sacrifice and, of course, she did both although she would not have acknowledged that she did either. Annie May simply did what she had to do - as she had done for over half a century.

The boy prospered. He passed from Standard One to Standard Two and onto Three automatically and Standard Four saw him recognised as scholarship potential.

Each June, the schools of the town enroled their best students in the Scholarship Lists. Selected pupils were placed in the groups befitting their status and were coached and crammed to fit the requirements of the examining board and be selected to enter the town's County School.

Annie May was invited to an appointment with the Headmaster - Mr. Eli Meyrick - at 2.45 ("that's a quarter to three 'en it?" she asked several of the neighbours) to discuss Charles' suitability.

She arrived neat and tidy in dress. Single minded in attitude. Had she not envisaged this day thirty years before?

The Master dominated her by his presence and Annie May dragged up her vision and her experience and her sacrifice and her industry in a single phrase when she said.

"Mr. Meyrick, I want what's best for the boy".

The boy was presented for the examination and Annie May made his life a misery - at least for the next two months.

"Have you done your homework?" she chided. "Let me see it. Go and fetch John from next door but one, to check what you've done".

This she did not know. That request cemented a friendship that lasted over fifty years. Charles never had a brother. He almost had a surrogate but, Plumduff returned to his London home and disappeared. Ruth, his half sister, had died and in any case would have been old enough to have been his mother, but John Pugh became his second self and distance nor time nor death could ever separate their brotherhood.

John had passed the scholarship four years earlier and knew the ropes. "Do it like this" he said. "You'll be OK. Heavy is to light" like "Large is to little. See?" said John and mostly Charles did.

Annie May stood back and used everyone, without guile, whom she saw as a means to fulfilment of that far away dream. "Surely" she said to herself as she lay alone in her marital bed, "God would not have revealed himself to me if there had been no purpose?"

Charles was entered, with a dozen more from his school, in the annual scholarship and waited, as everyone waited, for the results. Two months was a lifetime of uncertainty and dreams for the boy and two or three hundred more. But for

Annie May they were months of certainty. No way would her boy fail to pass the scholarship. Had not the firelight and the Trinity revealed the outcome years before? Charles would go to the County School as surely as the sun would bless tomorrow's dawn.

She was not wrong this time. The boy passed. High on the list.

That fact presented further problems. Uniforms, satchels, geometrical tools, rulers, pencils had to be provided. Annie May had not envisaged the cost that was way beyond her means to provide.

Annie May had put her young son to bed that June evening. She took pencil and paper and made a list:

It read:	Blazer	2 10s 0d
	Badge	6s 6d
	Trowsers	27s 6d
	Sachel	1 19s 6d
	Things to do his work	1s 0d
		5 19s 6d

Spelling did not come easy.

Nearly six pounds. Eight weeks widow's pension after paying the rent.

She thought of nothing else for days on end and sought advice of the one person who would know. Maggie opened her arms and her heart and explained how Annie May could get a bursary by going to the authorities and, pressed her to take two pounds - a loan if she wished, to help her out. It was all she could now afford for her children kept her at home and John's salary at the library was not great. Ten days later, with a fortnight to go before Charles' entry into education, two more pound notes were needed.

The answer was a product of human greed. "Those that have, always have on the back of the have nots", had been Harry's creed and Annie May used its philosophy to sacrifice her own - not her son's - clothing coupons to the wife of a certain business man for £1 10s 0d.

Charles set off to the County School on the appointed

September day, pleased with himself but unaware of the two blue eyes that followed his journey down the lane and the journey backwards that his "scholarship" conjured up in the mind of that simple lady.

Charles and his mother were both proud of the badge he sported on his blazer breast pocket. "County School" it said in neatly embroidered Roman capitals.

They had both arrived.

* * * * *

Annie May's journey had taken fifty three years. Her son's a mere eleven. The only common route was their fathers' ends. Hers a release, for The Rock's sake. His a time of afraidness and loneliness and lack! "Mam's great" that little boy thought "but she don't know about cricket. She can't add up and she can't read good. And she's deaf! And I hate her 'cos everyone else has everything they want and I haven't got nothing. I hate her".

Annie May looked at her son awake and sleeping and she knew that God's message at that special place had not been false.

On a Summer day in 1945 Annie May suggested a picnic. He did not really want to go because Mam was difficult. Well, he knew that she could not help being old fashioned and deaf. But it wasn't easy for that young boy.

They left No. 5 Bryn Bicca at ten o'clock in the morning. The sun had already announced its early warmth and, the old middle aged lady and her twelve year old, stepped from the house and both skipped down the stepping places to the lampost.

They turned left and followed the narrow track along Ike Caswell's field until a stile led them into a kind of freedom. Beyond Blue Lake with its miraculous water that served the greedy steel works, past water cress beds and rock outcrops, on and on to the mountains. Over each of them an awareness descended. To Annie May, a renewal. For the boy, a revelation. He could see four valleys between the crest knuckles of the mountain. Wales in all its paradox. He searched and scars appeared. Desolate mine workings and iron oxide clouds and for the first time in his young life he "saw" his mother.

Today had not been a picnic. True there were sandwiches and an apple but today was the day of understanding.

When they had finished the meagre meal, both were refreshed, although Charles was thirsty. Half a flask of stale tea hardly satisfied a healthy twelve year old. But other thirsts had intruded into his awareness. "She 'ent so daft" he said to himself. "I love you Mam" he said out loud. She did not hear it seemed.

Then they arrived at a lovely place. Tired old Mam sat down first and Charles explored a bit. He noticed that some streams ran down the hillside.

Mam had a few biscuits tucked away and Charles lay looking at the sun, that now sat high above, through closed eyes. He nibbled a NICE biscuit. Dots and squiggles and shadows and moving images and brilliances. Then the sun directed the undirected and the boy saw the streams joining and flowing and torrenting - and a vision was renewed.

"Charles" she called. "I call this place Trinity. I asked Martha Jane where it ended. She said the English Channel. She did not know the question".

"Son" she said holding the boy fiercely, "You are the end".

PUBLICATIONS BY BLORENGE BOOKS

Blorenge Books publish books about Wales and in particular the area covered by the ancient kingdom of Gwent. Copies of the following titles may be obtained by writing to Blorenge Books and enclosing cheques (made out to Blorenge Books) for the relevant amounts:-

Hando's Gwent Vol II by Chris Barber	£7.50
The Ancient Stones of Wales by Chris Barber & John Williams	£7.95
Journey to Avalon by Chris Barber & David Pykitt (hardback)	£15.75
The Seven Hills of Abergavenny by Chris Barber	£5.25
Shall We Meet Again? by Marguerite Shaw	£4.75
Stone and Steam in the Black Mountains by David Tipper	£5.75
Arthurian Caerleon by Chris Barber	£3.99
Portraits of the Past (Hardback) by Chris Barber and Michael Blackmore	£19.95

Blorenge Books, Blorenge Cottage, Church Lane, Llanfoist
Abergavenny NP7 9NG
Tel: 01873 856114

JOURNEY TO AVALON
by Chris Barber & David Pykitt

Hundreds of books have been written about King Arthur but the majority of them say nothing new. Journey to Avalon finally sorts out fact from fiction to provide the most convincing and detailed account of King Arthur and his times that has ever been compiled. Packed with illustrations and fascinating information, it is an intriguing work of historical detection in which the well known author Chris Barber and David Pykitt, an expert on Dark Age history, unlock the solution to one of the greatest mysteries in the world.

This fascinating book explains the importance of the historical links between South Wales, Cornwall and Brittany, providing the reasons why King Arthur is so well remembered in those areas. Fact is sometimes more remarkable than fiction.

ISBN 1-872730-03-5   Hardback £15.75.

THE ANCIENT STONES OF WALES
by Chris Barber & John Williams

This fascinating book provides an in-depth study of all the megalithic monuments of Wales. Erected by man in prehistoric times for some long forgotten purpose, the solitary standing stones, stone circles and dolmens are riddles in the landscape that seem to defy explanation. Illustrated with a profusion of photographs, the book includes a gazeteer of all the megalithic sites in Wales and contains some remarkable information which will astound and intrigue the reader.

Hardback £13.50 ISBN 0-9510444-6-X
Softback £7.95 ISBN 0-9510444-7-8

SHALL WE MEET AGAIN ?
by Marguerite Shaw

Marguerite Shaw tells the story of the life of Robbie Watkins, his family and friends, through war and peace, prosperity and adversity. She sets a wholly authentic scene for the Watkins family of whom many of her readers said, "I felt I knew everyone of them, I cried with them and laughed with them and I want to know what happens to them next".

Softback £4.75 ISBN 1-872730-01-9

HANDO'S GWENT VOLUME II
Edited by Chris Barber

Two volumes of Hando's Gwent have been published as a tribute to the work of Fred Hando, who as an artist/historian spent a lifetime exploring and recording the history, legends, architecture and scenery of an area he loved passionately.

It is fitting that Chris Barber should compile and edit the material for this series, for in his youth he accompanied Fred Hando on many of his travels and was much influenced by the experience. Everyone who loves this small but beautiful county will find the book fascinating. (Volume I is at present out of print).

Hardback £13.00   ISBN 0-9510444-4-3
Softback   £7.95 ISBN 09510444-5-1b

THE SEVEN HILLS OF ABERGAVENNY
By Chris Barber

This delightful book is a walking guide to the shapely summits that surround this historic market town situated on the edge of the Brecon Beacons National Park. A total of seventeen routes are included and the book is also packed with a wide assortment of fascinating history, legend and anecdotes which will be of interest to the casual visitor as well as the hill walker seeking a fresh challenge.

Softback   £5.25 ISBN 1-872730-02-7

'PORTRAITS OF THE PAST'
by Chris Barber & Michael Blackmore

Compiled by Chris Barber and illustrated by the well known artist Michael Blackmore, this book tells the story of the industrial history of Monmouthshire which at one time was one of the greatest iron producing areas in Britain.

Packed with beautiful and detailed illustrations, 'Portraits of the Past' provides a fascinating record of ironworks, tramroads, canals, collieries and railways established in this county during the days when, raw materials, engineering expertise and manpower were combined to produce a social and economic revolution.

It is a 'coffee table' book and in future years will be regarded as a much prized possession.

Hardback £19.95 ISBN 1-872730-05-1